ENTWINED
WITH YOU
J. KENNER

NEW YORK TIMES BESTSELLING AUTHOR

D1496354

"She said she loved you over and over. Not that she needed to say it. I could hear it in every word she said about you. Honestly, she was gooey with it. It was a little sickening," she added, but the goofy smile told him that it wasn't sickening at all. That she'd been happy for her twin.

"Then why—"

She held up a hand, cutting him off. "I believe she trusted you. I really do. But here's the thing, Braxton. Brent. *Benjamin*," she added, leaning forward as she spoke the birth name he hated. "And I want you to understand that I need to be honest with you."

"Well, yeah. Of course."

"She may have trusted you, but I don't. Not yet."

"What are you talking—"

"You're alive, Brax. You're alive because you weren't in the van when it blew up. So you tell me, Brax. Why the fuck would I ever trust you?"

Charismatic. Dangerous. Sexy as hell.
Meet the elite team of Stark Security.

For all JK titles, please visit
www.jkenner.com

PRAISE FOR J. KENNER'S NOVELS

"PERFECT for fans of *Fifty Shades of Grey* and *Bared to You. Release Me* is a powerful and erotic romance novel that is sure to make adult romance readers sweat, sigh and swoon." *Reading, Eating & Dreaming Blog*

"I will admit, I am in the 'I loved *Fifty Shades*' camp, but after reading *Release Me*, Mr. Grey only scratches the surface compared to Damien Stark." *Cocktails and Books Blog*

"It is not often when a book is so amazingly well-written that I find it hard to even begin to accurately describe it . . . I recommend this book to everyone who is interested in a passionate love story." *Romancebookworm's Reviews*

"The story is one that will rank up with the *Fifty Shades* and Cross Fire trilogies." *Incubus Publishing Blog*

"The plot is complex, the characters engaging, and J. Kenner's passionate writing brings it all perfectly together." *Harlequin Junkie*

"A sizzling, intoxicating, sexy read!!!! J. Kenner had me devouring Wicked Dirty, the second installment of *Stark World Series* in one sitting. I loved everything about this book from the opening pages to the raw and vulnerable characters. With her sophisticated prose, Kenner created a love story that had the perfect blend of lust, passion, sexual tension, raw emotions and love." *Michelle, Four Chicks Flipping Pages*

ENTWINED WITH YOU

J. KENNER

NEW YORK TIMES BESTSELLING AUTHOR

M&O

Entwined With You Copyright © 2023 by Julie Kenner

Excerpt from *Wicked Grind* © Copyright 2017 by Julie Kenner

Cover design by Michele Catalano, Catalano Creative

Cover image by Authorcuraphotography (depositphotos.com)

ISBN: 978-1-958379-13-4

Published by Martini & Olive Books

V-2023-8-20P1

PROLOGUE

I don't know him.

I can't trust him.

Not really. I have to remember. I have to play a part. Because no matter how much I might want him, I must keep the past firmly in mind. Must force myself to keep the truth I now live by firmly in my head. The truth that he could be the one who took Sabrina's wild light from this world....

How many times had he told her, "I love you?"

Had each kiss been a lie? Each promise a deception?

I don't know. And yet somehow, I must find out.

I have to be careful. I have to be smart.

I need to keep my distance.

I need to protect my heart.

I need to find the truth.

And above all else, I have to keep my own secrets locked away safe inside.

All sound advice. A good policy. A solid plan.

And yet I can't seem to follow my own edict. Because with every moment that passes, I sink deeper and deeper. And all I can do is hope that if I go under, he will be the one to pull me up to safety, and not the man who lets me drown.

CHAPTER ONE

September 2.

Braxton Reed stared at the date on the wall calendar, his ears ringing from the explosion, his skin hot from the flames engulfing the van across the intersection. *Sabrina.*

Oh, dear god, Sabrina.

The burning van. The concrete beneath him. His body aching from anguish and horror. *The woman behind the wheel.*

He tried to race forward, but he couldn't move. He couldn't see her. The world was swimming, blurring, and his throat ached from the force of his scream.

Over and over and over. Every—

"Brax? You with us?"

Ryan Hunter's voice cut through the roar in

his head, and Brax pinched the bridge of his nose, trying to force himself back to the present. To *this* September second. Not the one fifteen years ago. The one he relived every goddamn year.

"*Agent Reed.*" Ryan's voice was sharper now, concern hiding in the stern tone.

Brax shook his head, then drew a breath. With a shudder, he met his boss's vibrant blue eyes across the conference room table. "Sorry, sorry." He curled his toes in his shoes, a trick he used when the memories stole his focus. Across the table from him, Mason Walker tilted his head, and Brax thought he saw compassion. He turned away; compassion was something he neither wanted nor deserved. "Rough night," he lied, tossing out the first excuse he could think of. In fact, the night had been easy. Hard to have a rough one when you drank enough to keep all the demons away. Or tried to, anyway.

"Your work has been exemplary these last few months, Brax. You've been an excellent addition to Stark Security."

Brax swallowed, waiting for the *but*. It didn't come.

"That's why I'm putting you on as Omega Team Leader. Cami will be your second. Mason will head up Alpha team." He paused only briefly, but in the silence, Brax heard the words Ryan didn't say: *This is a test. I'm moving you up faster than usual. Don't let me down.*

"I appreciate that, sir. You can count on me." He meant the words, hating that this meeting had to happen today. He shouldn't have even come in. After so many years, he should know better. For him, September second should be a perpetual sick day.

"So what's the job?" Mason asked, running his fingers through his dark hair. "And why are we running an Alpha team with an Omega one?"

Brax didn't know the how or the why of it, but he knew that Mason had partial amnesia. The sane part of him knew that it was nuts for him to be envious of the man, but damned if that didn't sound like a dream to him. To be able to forget. Hell, even if he forgot his entire life, to be free of that one, horrible day...

"—explain that in a moment," Ryan was saying.

Brax pulled himself out of his thoughts, forcing his attention to the monitor mounted on the far wall of the conference room. As the Stark Security Agency logo rotated on screen,

Ryan began. "It may turn out to be nothing, but Kingston Wolfe reached out about some gemstones he acquired about twelve years ago."

"Kingston Wolfe," Brax repeated. "That name's familiar."

"I'm not surprised. He's the heir to the Carnell fortune. Some branch of the British royal family that made a killing in trade generations ago. Kingston moved to the States for college, and has managed to keep a low profile. He and Damien have sponsored a few charity fundraisers over the years," Ryan added, referring to Damien Stark, the tennis pro turned billionaire who had created Stark Security after the kidnapping of his youngest daughter.

"So what does Wolfe need us for?" Mason asked.

"He's loaning some gemstones to the Margaret Gleason Performing Arts Center. He wants extra security during the transfer and then our presence for the weekend that the gems are on display."

Brax shot a glance toward Mason, who answered the silent question with a shrug. Brax almost laughed, glad the two of them were on the same page. "And why exactly are gems being displayed at a performing arts center?"

Ryan pressed his fingers to his temples and shook his head. "No good reason I can think of, and I've spoken to both Margaret and Wolfe. But they're determined. Two of the most valuable gemstones on the planet. Stones that are supposedly cursed, no less. Even so, they're taking them out of the vault and putting them on a stage. It's a hell of a commission for us, but damned stupid on their part, especially since Wolfe is convinced there may be an attempt to steal the stones."

"Why the hell is he putting them on display if that's what he thinks?" Mason asked.

"And why does he think that?" Brax added. "Thieves don't usually pre-announce their intent."

"These stones toured before, years ago, before Wolfe acquired them. And there was an attempt back then. And since the announcement that they would be on display, we've heard some chatter about a possible jewel heist in LA."

Brax felt his body go cold. Surely Ryan wasn't talking about....

But no. Displaying those stones would be stupid beyond all imagining.

"There's no specific threat," Ryan said. "Just Wolfe's caution based on history. But because he's aware that he's just being cautious, he refuses to consider calling off the event. That's his prerogative." He looked to each man in turn. "Nothing will happen to those stones on our watch."

"No, sir," Mason said.

"No..." Brax said, the word coming slowly, as if from the past into which his mind had slipped.

"Alpha team will be in charge of overt security. Choose your team," he said to Mason. "As many as you deem necessary. The Center is giving us oversight of their in-house security as well. Make a plan and report back to me tomorrow."

"Will do," Mason said. "This will give me the chance to get to know the newbies better, too," he added, referring to several new agents who'd signed on in the last few weeks. Over the last few years, Stark Security had gained an excellent reputation and was growing fast. There was even talk about opening a Manhattan location to complement the current Los Angeles one, something Brax found intriguing, even though he was certain that living in that city would be like walking around with a wound that kept ripping back open.

"As for you," Ryan added, turning his attention to Brax, "I want you and Cami to do what you do best. Hit the streets. See if you can nail down this buzz about a diamond heist about to go down."

Brax nodded. He and Cami Green had worked together as undercover agents at the FBI, and when they'd come over to Stark Security, it was agreed that they'd continue to do covert operations when in the field. The agents at Stark Security knew who they were, of course, but no one outside the company knew that they were in any way affiliated with SSA. They even entered through the basement, accessing the building from a small office building over a block away.

He was about to ask about the original heist —which would, of course, be his and Cami's starting point—but Mason spoke first.

"Seriously. Why a performing arts center?"

"An opera," Ryan said.

Brax leaned back, arms crossed over his chest. "An opera?"

Ryan lifted his hands in a *who am I to question* gesture. "Apparently, someone's written an opera about these stones. It's the opening show for the center, and the first night will lead off with a gala where the actual gemstones will be on display—to be switched out later with some rather extraordinary counterfeits for purely decorative purposes.

"What do we know about the stones?"

Ryan clicked the remote, and the logo dissipated into a cloud of pixels as an image popped on screen. Brax gaped at the stunning blue stone encircled by diamonds. "Wolfe acquired the Hope Diamond?" How could he not have heard about that?

Ryan chuckled. "I did pick the right man for the job. I was about to ask if either of you recognized it. And no, it's only related to the gems we're interested in."

"I've heard the name, of course," Mason said. "Can't say I knew what it actually looked like."

"So what gems are we protecting?" The hair on the back of Brax's neck was standing up, and all he could do was pray that his Spidey-sense was wrong.

"The Sisters," Ryan said, clicking the remote again. The screen changed, this time showing two smaller, but equally blue diamonds in intricate settings. One as a ring, the other a necklace.

Brax swallowed, his stomach going sour. *This couldn't be happening.*

"Sisters?" Mason asked.

"Believe it or not, the stone the Hope Diamond was cut from was significantly bigger. I think it was Louis XIV who had it cut down, and for centuries, people wondered what happened to the parts that were trimmed off. Experts believed that nothing happened—that there'd been no way to salvage the removed pieces. They sited various reasons having to do with the cut and the available tools, none of which is relevant to us."

"But apparently those experts were wrong," Brax said.

Ryan nodded. "Apparently. A few gemologists had put forth a process of cutting the Hope Diamond down that would be difficult but feasible. But since no one had ever seen these possible cut stones, everyone assumed that theoretical possibility was never put into practice."

"And then the Sisters showed up," Brax said.

"Exactly. About fifteen years ago, the previous owner went public about the Sisters, saying that had been in his family for centuries. He had the provenance, too. Specifically, centuries-old notes showing when and how the Sisters were cut from the Hope Diamond."

"Must have caused a flutter among gem enthusiasts," Mason said even as Brax tried to fight a rising wave of nausea.

"Oh, yes. And of course, the entire world wanted to see them. A tour was scheduled, with the first stop being the Los Angeles Natural History Museum. But there was an attempted theft before the exhibit even opened, and one of the potential thieves was killed."

"One of?" Mason asked. "The rest were captured? How big was the team?"

"Five," Ryan said. "One died in an explosion during the attempted heist. One has never been found. Three were caught and incarcerated. All three were paroled but only two are still living."

"And that's where we come in," Brax said, forcing the words out past the rising bile, hoping his forehead wasn't sweating.

"Exactly," Ryan said.

Mason frowned. "And there've been no other attempts since the one fifteen years ago?"

"No. The original owner canceled the tour and never displayed them again. He held onto them a few years, but apparently he went a little mad believing they were cursed."

"So he sold them to Wolfe," Mason said.

Ryan nodded. "This is the first time the Sisters will be seen outside the vault in Wolfe's home. Naturally, he wants to be careful. Brax?"

Brax blinked, realizing he was clutching his stomach and standing. "Sorry. Queasy." He turned and ran out of the conference room, barely noticing the way the other agents and staff in the bullpen gaped as he moved like a rocket to the men's room. He threw himself into a stall, bent over, and vomited up last night's liquid dinner and bile.

Fucking September second.

He stood carefully, then leaned his cheek against the metal wall, his eyes closed and his throat burning. He waited, listening, but no one else had come in. He said a silent thanks to his co-workers. Nice to work with people who knew when to give you space.

Feeling shaky, he left the stall and went to a sink to splash water on his face. He drew a breath, then clutched the marble counter as he stared at the mirror and into his own eyes. The eyes of man who back then had called himself

Brent Travers. A man who'd been lost and stupid and in love with a girl named Sabrina.

She'd died for those goddamn stones.

And now he was going to have to protect them.

Fifteen years ago

"Second thoughts?" Brent looked at her from the van's passenger seat. Her posture was relaxed, but her hands were gripped tight enough that her knuckles were white.

Sabrina gave him an eye roll as she turned to face him. "You know me better than that. I'm fine. Just some pre-op jitters."

"You?" He almost laughed. She was right; he did know her well. And on a job, she was as cold as ice and utterly fearless. If she was nervous now...

He reached for her, relieved when she immediately took one hand off the steering wheel and entwined her fingers with his. "Why jitters?"

"I don't—" She cut herself off with a shake of her head. "Okay, yesterday, I ... never mind. It's stupid. I just got spooked."

"What happened?"

"Nothing." She squeezed his hand, then pulled her fingers free. She ran them through her hair, something she always did when she trying to avoid something.

"Brina, come on. It's me. What spooked you?"

"Nothing." She snapped the word out. "It's just the job. This is huge. And we've never worked with Darrin or Jorge or Tim before. I've got a right to be nervous don't I?"

"Sure. Of course." He wasn't sure what to think. He'd never seen her nervous. She was always ultra gung-ho for every job. He was just about to say something—he didn't know what—when she reached for his hand again.

"I'm sorry. I'm not used to being nervous and it's making me edgy." She shrugged, then lifted their joined hands to her lips and kissed his knuckles. "Maybe it's because I have so much to lose now."

She met his eyes as she spoke, but she didn't hold them. Instead, they dropped away, as if she wasn't sure she should have said that.

"Oh, baby." He cupped her head, then leaned over to kiss her softly, but she pulled him close in a kiss that was anything but soft. On the contrary, it was wild. Almost desperate. And he would have given anything to let it go on and on and on.

But they couldn't.

They had a job to do.

He broke the kiss and was shocked to see tears snaking down her cheeks. "Dammit, Brina, what's going on? And don't lie to me."

He watched as she composed herself. As she drew in two breaths and let them out slowly. As she sat up straighter. As she smiled, just a little too broadly, then wiped a finger under each eye. "I told you. It's nothing—"

"Oh, for fuck's sake," he snapped. "This is *me*, Brina. Just fucking tell me."

"It's *nothing*," she repeated, this time holding up a hand to keep him silent. "I just—I don't know. I just have a bad feeling." He watched as her body shook, like a small jolt of electricity had cut through her.

"Baby, why?" He took her hands in his.

"I don't know. Everything's on track. We've rehearsed this so much we could pull it off in our sleep. Everything's in place. We've got solid partners. It's the perfect plan." Her shoulders rose and fell. "Dammit, I feel stupid."

"Stupid?" She wasn't making sense.

"I had a bad dream last night, okay? I dreamt the mission went south. It made me edgy, and I didn't want to tell you because it was just a dream. A stupid, fucking dream."

He frowned, looking around the area. Feeling suddenly like a sitting duck.

"If you have a bad feeling, we don't have to do this. We can walk. We can just turn around and walk. Hitch our way across the country. Clean rooms on a cruise ship so we can get to Italy. We could start a whole new life."

A smile tugged at the corner of her mouth. "Neither one of us speaks Italian. And we already said we were quitting. We're quitting after this job. When we'll have the cash to afford to live."

He nodded. She was right. This job was a means to an end. They had it all planned out. Hell, they even had documents ready to go for their new names. And their take would be enough to last a lifetime. Pretty sweet considering neither of them had ever held a real job or had actual life skills. Oh, sure, they had *skills*. But somehow forgery, lock picking, and hacking security systems weren't the kind of things potential employers looked for.

"All right," he said. "We do the job. We follow the plan."

She grinned. "Good."

"I just have one little condition."

She tilted her head, one brow rising. "Oh, really?"

"Kiss me," he said, his heart swelling at the sight of her slow, sexy smile.

"Well," she said breezily, as she shifted on the van's old bench seat to face him. "I suppose if you insist."

The kiss was sweet and long and not nearly enough. It was interrupted by the chime of the timer on his phone.

They broke apart, holding each other's gaze. Then he lifted her hand to his lips and kissed her fingers. "To be continued," he said, making her laugh out loud.

As he opened the passenger door, she started the van. He got out into the unseasonable Los Angeles heat and started walking the toward the museum as she waited in the parallel parking spot, ready to take off when the time was right.

He told himself that he believed her; that nothing was wrong. But the knot in his stomach suggested that he was lying to himself. Maybe she was just growing up. Maturing. Realizing they weren't invincible, and that was triggering nerves.

But he didn't believe it. They'd both stared down their own mortality years ago. She'd always faced risks, and she'd always flipped risk the bird.

As far as Sabrina was concerned, the entire world was one big playground that existed only to amuse her. It was that attitude—carefree, defiant, and utterly competent—that had drawn him to her six years ago. He'd just turned fourteen. She'd been a few months away, just three months younger than him. Somehow, though, she'd seemed older, and centuries wiser. *An old soul.* That's how Theo, the shelter's brawny director who looked more like a thug than a social worker, had described her the first time she walked into the Manhattan shelter, and Brent had to agree.

He'd sucked up his courage, then walked across the shelter's recreation area to introduce himself. Exactly nine minutes later, he was head-over-heels in love. Now they were both twenty, had been through hell and back together, and he still felt exactly the same thing.

And the best part? She did, too.

From that first day—hell, from that first minute—they could tell each other anything. And they did. They'd sat on the mats in the north corner of the rec room and talked for hours. It sounded corny as hell, but he knew he'd found the rest of himself. Like he'd been half-empty before she'd walked through those doors.

They never kept secrets. Never held back.

At least, they never had before.

Today, something was wrong. Trying to convince himself otherwise was just so much nonsense.

She was nervous, and he didn't have a clue why.

He reached the museum and circled around to his designated spot, close enough to receive the transmission from the team inside the building, and still within the range where he could signal Brina to bring the van to the meeting point.

Just a few more minutes, and they'd be hauling ass out of here, only days away from selling the merchandise and then taking their share of the money and retiring.

With a sigh of eager anticipation, he glanced across the intersection toward the van, frustrated that the sun's glare meant he couldn't see her behind the wheel.

He shifted, trying to find a better angle, then took a single step to his right.

And that was it.

He froze in horror as the world exploded, his ears ringing, his heart pounding, his entire body ravaged by shock and grief as he heard her voice in his head, firm and sweet. *Run, dammit. Run!*

CHAPTER TWO

"Oh, I don't think that sequence was unrealistic at all," Brax said to Trevor Barone as they sat around a poolside table on Damien Stark's massive back porch.

"Uh-huh," Trevor said. "Were we in the same theater?" The two of them and Ollie McKee, Trevor's boyfriend, had come straight to the party from seeing a newly released action movie.

Brax kept his expression deadpan. "No, really. Absolutely realistic." He shot a sideways glance toward Ollie, one of the guests of honor at this celebratory party. "Ollie and I scaled the outside of skyscrapers at least weekly back in the day." He kept his voice as even as if he were reporting the weather.

"Typical day at the FBI, right, Ol? I mean, if weapons were being trafficked, we'd do whatever it took to get them out of the wrong hands."

"Oh, totally," Ollie said as he turned toward Trevor, his mouth twitching as he fought not to smile. Brax and Ollie had become fast friends at the Academy before going their separate ways. Ollie was still in the FBI, but Brax had left to join Stark Security, where Trevor also worked as an agent.

Brax kept his face serious as he met Trevor's brown eyes, so dark they were almost black. "Usually we'd scale a building or two the same day we Halo jumped onto the roof of various foreign corporations from Dubai to Berlin to Moscow. I'll say this much—working for the FBI really kept me in good shape."

"Wow," Trevor said, his voice cracking from the effort to hold back laughter. "And here I thought the FBI only had domestic jurisdiction."

Brax shot Ollie a conspiratorial grin. "Well, there's jurisdiction, and then there's *jurisdiction*. And we only let a few trusted colleagues in on our secrets. Of course, if you tell anyone, we will have to kill you."

Ollie shrugged, then put his arm around Trevor's shoulder. "Sorry, babe. Rules are rules."

"What on earth are you guys talking about?" Jamie Hunter asked coming up from behind Brax, the loose waves of her dark-brown hair framing the kind of face that made a camera lens giddy. She glanced around at all of them. "Tell me it's not a new case."

"New movie," Brax said. "Bullshit ending."

Trevor laughed, leaning in closer to Ollie. "Well, they can't all be as happy as ours."

"True that," Brax said, his smile genuine as he shot Trevor a nod of thanks. After Brax had emerged from his breakdown in the men's room earlier that afternoon, he'd noticed Trevor and Mason chatting by the door of the conference room. A moment later, Trevor had come over and announced that he was going to talk Ollie into playing hooky for the rest of the day, and that Brax should join them for the latest action blockbuster.

Brax had almost declined. He'd wanted to tell Trevor and Mason and Ryan and anyone else who'd been paying attention that he didn't need to be handled. He was fine. Perfectly fine.

Except he hadn't been fine. Not then.

He'd been a fucking wreck, as every single

person in the office could see. Option number two had been to tell Trevor that he was going to pack up and go home early. Get his head in order. But somehow, the words hadn't come.

Except for those years with Sabrina, Brax had always been a loner. Working with her had changed that. He'd loved the give-and-take. The planning. Loved celebrating when they'd scored and commiserating when they hadn't. He'd even loved getting close to the marks as they worked a con. Enjoyed it enough, in fact, that he started to feel bad when the con paid off.

Sabrina had felt the same, and they'd shifted their *modus operandi*. Less grift, more sticky fingers and forgery and online access to things he really shouldn't have access to. Like, oh, security systems. But oh how the money had rolled in.

He still valued solitude, but at the same time, he genuinely liked working with and around people. As a child, he never would have expected it. People—especially his parents and cousins—weren't to be trusted. But starting with Brina and continuing later with Ollie at the Academy, he'd come to learn that it wasn't his innate personality that wanted to pull a Greta Garbo; it was the little boy trapped inside who'd been hurt so badly so many times.

And so he'd said yes to Trevor and the movies, then joined them at this party in celebration of the successful conclusion of a recent kidnapping case. Originally, he'd intended to beg off. Now, he was glad he hadn't.

"Anybody need a drink?" he asked pushing back from the table.

"I'll take a whiskey," Ollie said. "But I can come with you."

Brax waved the words away. "I'll get it. Anyone else?"

No one else chimed in, so Brax started to head back in the direction Jamie had come from, his gaze taking in the incredible view of the sun setting over the Pacific as well as the clusters of people scattered around the deck of the infinity pool. Most of the guests were Stark Security Agents and their significant others, but there were also a few friends of the Starks, their live-in nanny, and even a smattering of kids running around.

Damien and his wife, Nikki, a former beauty queen with a smile as wide as her native state of Texas, approached, drinks in hand. "Glad you made it," Damien said as they passed, and Brax wondered if Ryan had told Damien—who was Ryan's business partner and best friend—about Brax's meltdown. Surprisingly, the possibility didn't piss him off. On the contrary, it made him feel warm and welcome, as if the people around him genuinely cared. For the first time it truly hit him: He'd found a home at Stark Security.

A home.

He'd never had that before. Certainly not with his parents, and not even with Sabrina. *She'd* been his home, true. Wherever he was with her, was wherever he was supposed to be. But they'd never had a place that was warm and welcoming. Never had a door he looked forward to unlocking. Never had any location to put down roots.

And for the last fifteen years, he hadn't even had her.

Now, though...

Well, maybe, just maybe, he finally had a place to call home. After all, it was still fucking September second, and he wasn't at home getting drunk and watching and re-watching *Kill Bill*, which had been the last movie they'd rented and watched together.

Maybe miracles did happen. Maybe time really did heal all wounds.

Or maybe he'd just become numb.

He paused a few yards from the bar when he felt his phone vibrate in his back pocket. He pulled it out, then froze when he saw the text on his screen.

I hope this is the right number. I'm looking for Brent Travers. My name is Samantha—I'm Sabrina's sister.

I know who killed her. And I need your help to nail the bastard.

Brax glanced at his watch before climbing out of his Jeep. He'd parked on the street behind a baby blue VW Bug, rather than bother waiting for the terminally slow gate to the parking structure to open. After all, he was only running into the apartment long enough to change clothes, then heading back out again to meet Samantha at Blacklist, the nearby Venice Beach bar that they'd agreed to in their text messages.

Samantha.

There'd been a wreck on PCH, and it had taken him almost an hour to get home from

Damien's house. Throughout the entire coastal
drive his mind had spun with questions. He'd
wanted to actually talk with her on the phone—
had even suggested as much—but she'd insisted
on waiting until they met in person. She'd
immediately agreed to his suggestion of Blacklist, and then she'd disappeared, not even
acknowledging his text that he'd be there by
nine.

It was eight-thirty now, but the bar was only
a short walk from his apartment. He'd been
living in Venice Beach since he'd moved to LA a
few months ago. At the time, he'd promised
himself he'd keep his eyes open for a house, but
that had been a lie. A house meant putting
down roots, and it had been fifteen years since
he'd given a fuck about a wife, a house, two-
point-five kids, or any of the trappings of
normalcy.

He was living legit now, not even a
smidgeon on the grift. And that was about as
normal as he ever intended to be.

Once upon a time, though...

He sighed as he climbed the stairs to his
apartment, his mind whirling as he remembered
the plans he and Sabrina used to spin during
long nights in various shelters or while they

were snuggled together in a sleeping bag. And for those last two years—when they'd actually scored an apartment, well, then they'd truly been playing at domesticity. And it really hadn't sucked.

He'd wanted more. Hell, he'd wanted it all. Sabrina. A house with a yard. A dog. Maybe a cat. Probably a goldfish. And, yeah, even kids. One day he wanted kids.

No. He'd wanted *her* kids.

He'd wake up in the morning from dreams of a normal life, like normal people, with normal jobs after which they'd come home and eat normal meals in front of the television before making love in their normal bed, falling asleep in each other's arms, then starting the whole normal routine over the next morning.

Heaven.

At least in his head. Some part of him always wondered if they would have been happy like that. Or if one or the other of them needed the rush that came with the grift. Or, as he was now learning, the rush that came from chasing those grifters.

His was the third door on the second-story balcony that ran the length of the beach-facing apartments. He paused, his fingers poised over the keypad lock. He exhaled, then let his fore-head drop against the cool, painted surface of the door as he tried to fight the wave of melancholy.

It had been fifteen years since he lost her, and all that bullshit about time healing all wounds was just that—bullshit.

The wounds hadn't healed at all. Hell, they'd barely scabbed over in all this time. And now out of the blue some sister she'd never even mentioned had burst into his life and ripped the scab right off his flesh.

And on September second, too, just so he'd feel double the pain.

He couldn't do this. Not tonight. Not when he was already so raw. He should text her back. Tell her he had to go into work. Make plans to meet over lunch, just so he'd have a solid excuse to cap it at one hour in case the whole Meet The Sister thing was just too damn painful.

Of course it would be too damn painful.

Yeah, that's what he would do. He'd post-pone it. Give himself time to get his head together.

He pushed back from the door and was about to tap in the key code when a movement down the balcony caught his eye. He turned, and his heart stopped.

Sabrina?

She was in the shadows cast by the building next door, so he could barely see her face. Her hair was long, hanging in waves that fell past her shoulders, unlike the pixie cut she used to sport. It was red, too. The natural, gorgeous auburn that he'd rarely seen because she'd hid it with a Miss Clairol basic brown, stolen from whatever local drugstore was near their current flop.

It couldn't be. It couldn't.

But it was.

Somehow, it was really her.

He took a tentative step toward her. "Sabrina?"

She eased forward, putting her face in the light, and his breath caught in his throat. He heard himself make a small noise, somewhere between a gasp and as cry, then realized he was stumbling forward.

As he reached for the railing to steady himself, she raced toward him, catching his hand at the same time that his fingers closed around the rail. He felt the shock of connection —a frisson of sensuality that cut all the way to his core.

"Sabrina?"

She drew her hand away, her lips moving as she whispered something.

It took him a moment to realize that the word she was repeating over and over was, "sorry."

"Sabrina," he said again, stepping closer, seeing nothing but her face. Feeling nothing but the thickness of the air between them, the horrible inches that were keeping them apart. "Baby, how—?"

Her lips parted as if to answer, but he didn't wait to hear. He wasn't thinking anymore. *It was her.* And before she had a chance to utter even one single word, he pulled her into his arms, pressed his lips to hers, and kissed her.

He moaned, losing himself in the feel of her. In the certainty that the last fifteen years had been nothing but a horrible, awful nightmare from which he was finally waking.

And then she pushed away.

He stood there. Lost. Lonely. And horribly confused. "Sab—"

"No." She pressed her fingertip to his lips, cutting off the name. "I'm so, so sorry." Tears clung to her eyelashes. "I should have told you

in the text. I should have called first. I shouldn't
have done it like this."

His head was spinning. "What are you
talking—"

"I'm not her," she said, the words so hard
and fast that they silenced him with the effi-
ciency of a butcher knife.

She stepped backward, her head down, her
hands sliding into the pockets of her jeans
before she slowly lifted her head. He saw the
apology in the deep green eyes. "I'm not her,
Mr. Reed. Mr. Travers. Mr. Whoever You'll Be
Tomorrow."

He took a step back, only to realize there
was nowhere else to go. He'd already moved
away as she'd been speaking, and now his back
was pressed against the door. "What are you
talking about?"

"Exactly what I said in the text. I'm her
sister. I'm Samantha." She lifted a shoulder in a
tiny shrug. "I should have also told you that
we're identical twins."

CHAPTER THREE

N one of this was registering.

Or, more accurately, he could feel the inevitable truth bubbling up under the surface. But he didn't want to hear it. He wanted the version of reality that had flashed before his eyes, like the mini-movie you supposedly see before death. Only this would be in defiance of death and in celebration of life.

Her life.

Except it wasn't really her.

How the hell could it not really be her?

"Her sister," he said numbly.

She pulled her hands out of her pockets and smoothed them down her denim-clad thighs. "Listen, maybe this isn't a good time. I—I should give you time to settle. We can talk tomorrow."

"*No.*" The word burst out of him. If she left now, he might never find her again, and he couldn't lose her. Not now.

He drew in a breath, then said more calmly. "No, please stay. I need—" He cut himself off with a shake of his head, unable to get the words out past the ache in his chest. In his heart.

He closed his eyes, then tried again. "I lost her fifteen years ago, and it just about killed me. I know you're not her—I know that. But you're a connection."

He held up his hand, showing the silver ring in the shape of an Ouroboros, noticing how her eyes widened at the sight.

"You're wearing her ring." Her voice was barely a whisper. "I—I was with her when she got that ring."

"Just a few months before she ran away, right?"

Samantha nodded, her eyes bright as she blinked too fast. "She was thinking about suicide," she said, telling him the horrible truth that he already knew. "She said it would be okay because life and death formed a circle. All part of the whole."

"But she couldn't do it," Brax said. He knew the story well. She loved life too much. Maybe it was all a circle, but she hadn't made the journey around yet. She wanted so desperately to live, but—"

"But there wasn't anyway to live with our father." Her already pale skin lost the last remnants of color. "She ran away." She licked her lips, then swallowed. "She got away from him."

He studied her face, wondering if she'd stayed behind. And if so, why. But he couldn't ask. It didn't matter how familiar her face was; he didn't know this woman.

Instead, he held up the ring again. "This is all I have of hers, and now out of the blue you're here. You came for a reason, Samantha. Tell me why. Come inside or we can talk at Blacklist like we planned, but don't leave. Not today. Not on September second when I'm drowning in memories. When I can still hear the explosion. Please," he continued, forcing his voice not to shake. "Please stay. Even if all we do tonight is talk about our memories of her."

He watched her face—that face he used to know in such intimate detail that he could read every nuance, every tiny change in mood.

Except it wasn't Sabrina's face—not really.

And he had no idea what the woman standing in front of his door was thinking.

Finally, she nodded, her eyes flicking up to meet his as she did. "We can stay here." She bit her lower lip, then drew in a long breath before adding, "I—I'm not sure I can get through this conversation without crying, so I'd just as soon not be in public."

He nodded. "Understood," he said, as unlocked the door and ushered her inside. He followed, then shut the door. They both stood awkwardly in the small entryway that opened onto the also small living/dining area.

"Do you want a drink?" he finally asked, since he had no idea what else to say.

"Yeah. I think I need one." The corner of her mouth quirked up, and his heart stuttered when he saw Sabrina's familiar dimple on Samantha's cheek. *What the hell was he walking into?*

"Are you sure you're okay?" She took a tentative step toward him, her brow furrowed with concern.

He took a corresponding step back. "Yeah. I'm fine. It's just—"

"I know."

"—you look like her," he said, speaking over

her. His words were soft. Barely audible. But he knew she understood.

"I'm sorry." She didn't meet his eyes.

He drew a breath, confusion mixing with guilt. "No. You don't have anything to apologize for. We're both—well, I guess we're both hurting." That was true, but it was still hard to look at her, so he turned away to walk toward the kitchen. "I've got mixers. You want a G&T?"

He cringed. Gin and Tonic had been Sabrina's drink. But she answered right away, telling him that sounded great. If she understood why the question was awkward, she didn't show it.

The kitchen was separated from the dining area by a breakfast bar. She stood by the counter to fix their drinks. He mixed hers the way Sabrina had liked it, shocked he actually had a few scrawny limes in his fridge for garnish.

He passed her the drink, then poured himself two fingers of bourbon, neat. His back was to her, and he closed his eyes for just a moment to gather himself before turning to face her again.

He should have taken longer.

She'd taken a seat at the breakfast bar, both hands curled around the glass, her elbows on the faux granite. Her head was tilted to the left, her hair on that side hanging down, while the other side was tucked behind her ear.

He froze, unsure if he was in the now, or if he'd somehow fallen backward into the past. Sabrina had never seen this apartment, much less been in it, and yet he knew that pose. The way she held her glass, the way she tilted her head. Those green eyes that missed nothing, taking everything in.

Brina.

He heard a soft noise, like a startled gasp, then realized it came from him.

She straightened, her body stiffening and losing that sense of being utterly comfortable in the moment. "Are you okay?"

He nodded. "I—I was about to ask you why you didn't tell me you were alive. Why you waited so many years."

Her eyes widened as she leaned back, and he felt like an ass for saying that out loud.

"Then I remembered you're not her," he added quickly, silently ordering himself to get his shit together. "I'm sorry. This is harder than I expected. And you look so damn much like her...."

"Not my hair," she said. "She dyed hers,"

and for some reason the statement made him laugh.

She joined in, and for a moment, it was all fine. Strange, but fine.

Then the laughter died, and once again she asked if he would prefer that she leave. "It might be easier if you sleep on it. We could meet somewhere for breakfast."

"Do you really think I'll be able to sleep tonight?"

"You miss her that much."

It wasn't a question, but he answered anyway. "I miss her more than I could ever say."

"And you really loved her." Again, the words were flat, and he couldn't tell if she was speaking to him or herself. Or maybe to the universe at large.

"Desperately," he said. "I'll always love her."

"Our father always said he loved us, too. Some days, I even believed him. It didn't matter. Even if it was true, it didn't matter." She shrugged. "That's what they say, isn't it? You always hurt the ones you love?"

"Just because they say it—whoever the hell *they* are—doesn't make it true." He heard the edge in his voice. Sabrina had told him about her father—most of it, anyway. And there were

no parallels between him and that vile man
at all.

"Besides," Brax added. "He didn't. Love her,
I mean. Not from what Brina told me. That son-
of-a-bitch didn't love her at all."

Samantha's shoulder rose and fell, but other
than that, she made no comment. For a moment,
silence hung between them, and though he
knew it was rude, he used the time to study her
face—a face she shared with Brina. A face he
knew so damn well.

"And yes," he said, leaving the kitchen with
his drink as he headed for the sofa, nodding for
her to follow him. "I truly loved her." He'd loved
her so much he still wasn't over her. How many
friends had tried to set him up over the years?
Enough that he'd tired of the constant pressure.
He didn't want anyone else. How could he?
Brina had been his soulmate. She'd known all
his secrets. Had shared the darkest part of his
life. A part he still had to keep buried.

He'd had a few one-night stands. Even a
short-term friends-with-benefits arrangement
with Cami, who along with Ollie had been his
closest friend at the Academy. That arrangement, thankfully, had ended well before they'd
both been recruited by Stark Security. They

were still friends—hell, she was his best friend —and she knew more than anyone about his past.

But even Cami didn't know everything. Neither did Ollie, who'd confided so much to Brax. Neither did Ryan or Damien, even though both men seemed to have unlimited resources to dig out the truth about anyone.

The secret was his alone. The secret of a life he'd buried. A dark life he'd shared only with Brina.

He could never truly be with someone else because he could never truly *be*.

"Did I lose you?" She'd taken a seat at the other end of the sofa, and was sitting with her back against the armrest, one leg tucked beneath her and her drink balanced on her knee.

He shook himself back to reality. "Sorry. I'm in a little bit of shock here." He swept out his arm, indicating her. "Why didn't she tell me? About you, I mean. We shared everything. Or at least, I thought we had." Could he have misjudged their relationship so completely? She'd been his life. She was home and hearth and laughter and—

He closed his eyes as if that would shut off the pain in his heart. When he opened them again, he looked straight at that achingly familiar face. "Why?" he repeated. "I thought…"

"You thought she loved you," Samantha said, her voice almost a whisper.

The knife in his heart twisted a little. "Are you saying she didn't?"

For a moment, she was perfectly still, perfectly silent. Then she shook her head. "No, I'm not saying that at all. Are you saying that you had no secrets either? Nothing you kept completely to yourself?"

He thought about it, then shook his head. "I —no. No, I didn't. She was everything to me."

"Really?" Sam leaned back, her expression suggesting that he must be either a liar of a fool. "No secrets at all?"

"None." The word came quick, but after he said it, he leaned back and truly turned the question over in his mind. "No," he repeated. "No secrets. Maybe there were things about me she didn't know, but that was oversight, not something I kept hidden. And we talked about our families a lot. I mean, at first, that was what the core of what we had in common, you know? The families—the situations—that we'd escaped."

He bent over, his elbows on his knees as he

dragged his fingers through his hair. "I told her the truth. I always told her the truth." He lifted his head to once again meet Samantha's eyes. "I thought she always told me the truth, too."

"She did," Samantha said gently as tears pooled in her eyes. "I'm sure she did. About everything but me." She swept her index fingers under her eyes, catching the tears before they fell. "Don't hate her, Brax. She was only trying to protect me."

"Protect you? From me?" He shook his head, trying to make sense of the words. "You're saying she didn't trust me?"

"No. She did. She trusted you more than anyone."

It took a moment for her words to register, but when they did, he shifted on the sofa, his body stiffening as he went on full alert. "How do you know that?"

"She—we talked. We stayed in touch. Not every day. Not even every week. But we had a system for contacting each other. And she told me how much she loved you. How much she trusted you. The last time we talked, she said you were the best thing that had ever happened to her, and that soon you'd be living straight. Off the grift, and all that."

"She said that? What else did she say?"

"Nothing specific. Just that you had something big going, and afterward, you'd have enough to settle somewhere and start a real life. Get real jobs. She even talked about kids, and how you had to get clean if you were going to have the kind of family you both wanted. A family that wasn't run on lies and anger and pain."

He blinked, ignoring his own tears that snaked down his cheeks. "She told you that?"

Samantha nodded. "Yeah. She did. And she said she loved you over and over. Not that she needed to say it. I could hear it in every word she said about you. Honestly, she was gooey with it. It was a little sickening," she added, but the goofy smile told him that it wasn't sickening at all. That she'd been happy for her twin.

"Then why—"

She held up a hand, cutting him off. "I believe she trusted you. I really do. But here's the thing, Braxton. Brent. *Benjamin*," she added, leaning forward as she spoke the birth name he hated. "And I want you to understand that I need to be honest with you."

"Well, yeah. Of course."

"She may have trusted you, but I don't. Not yet."

"What are you talking—"

"You're alive, Brax. You're alive because you weren't in the van when it blew up. So you tell me, Brax. Why the fuck would I ever trust you?"

CHAPTER FOUR

M y words seem to hang in the air between us, and I sit up straighter, making a point of meeting his eyes without flinching. I expect him to yell at me. To toss excuses at me. To do anything and everything to convince me that he isn't a man who once killed the woman he loved.

But he doesn't say anything. Instead, I watch as his shoulders sag. As silence lingers between us. His head drops, and for a moment —one terrifying, beautiful moment—I see the depth of the danger I'm opening myself up to here. Because this is a man I want to trust. A man that a girl named Sabrina had loved with all her heart.

But I'm smarter than that girl. That foolish, dead girl.

I know better than anyone how few people truly reflect who they are inside. Everyday, we're walking through a world of strangers. On a subway. At work. Taking a kid to school. Having lunch with your gal pals.

No one's ever really who you see.

I didn't used to know that. Now, I know it only too well.

It's a hard lesson, and an unpleasant one. But once you wrap your head around it, the world is so much simpler because there's only one rule. One inviolate truth. A truth that makes the world a hell of a whole lot easier to navigate.

Don't trust anyone.

I lean forward, "What's the matter?" I press. "Taking longer than you expected to conjure a few fake tears?"

He lifts his head, and though I'm expecting fury, all I see is pain in his hazel eyes.

"Do you think I don't feel like it was my fault every single day?" His voice is soft and heavy. As if he's traveled back those fifteen years and is now pushing the words out from that great distance. "I didn't kill her. But I still have to remind myself of that every minute of every day."

I hear the pain in his voice, but I'm not moved. He drags his fingers through his hair, his face appearing to have aged twenty years in the last twenty seconds. "Do you think a moment goes by where I don't go over all the what-ifs in my head? I would have been in that van with her if I'd only ignored the damn text. Maybe I would have seen something. Heard something. Gotten us both out."

I frown. Text? This is new. But is it real or is it bullshit? Considering who I'm sitting across from, I'm guessing it's bullshit.

I want to ignore it; I'm sure he's just baiting me. But then I hear myself asking, "What text?" And in the space between my question and his answer, I feel the unwelcome flutter of hope's soft wings.

For years, I've believed that he was complicit. Maybe he didn't place the bomb, but he knew. Dammit, he *knew*. He knew and he stood there on the sidewalk as the last seconds of life ticked away from the woman he loved. He didn't raise a gun or pull a knife or strangle her in bed one hot and humid evening. But he was still just as guilty.

He stood there. He knew.

And because he didn't do a goddamn thing, she's dead now. Gone from the world. Erased completely, without even a buried body or a memorial stone. Just one simple death certificate filed in Los Angeles County. One piece of paper to mark the passing of a life that was stolen from her.

"What text," I repeat. "What are you talking about?"

He drags his fingers through his hair. "Sabrina told you about the heist?"

I force myself to meet his eyes when I answer. "She told me everything. Or," I add, "at least she said she did."

"Then you know that she and I had a couple of jobs. One had to do with the getaway."

"Go on."

"One of the guys was in a car near the service entrance to the museum. And once Darrin and the inside team got the Sisters, they'd leave through that entrance and get into the car."

"I know," I say. "It was all worked out. Security system circumvented. That was you and Brina. Everyone would go in as cleaners or security personnel. Once the security system was off, Darrin and Tim would replace the stones with counterfeit. You and Brina would be out by then. You'd ditch your security uniforms and get to the van."

The plan runs through my head like a movie. "Meanwhile, the guy driving the getaway car—what was his name?"

"Jorge."

"Right. He'd be on a street nearby. It was all timed, so he'd pull up and Darrin and Tim would slide in. Then Jose—"

"Jorge," he corrects.

"Sorry. Of course." I know the name just fine. But Samantha probably wouldn't have. "Anyway, *Jorge* would get out of there. Except it wasn't the only getaway car. There was the van."

"Keep going."

"Jorge would drop Darrin at the van with one of the sisters. That way the gems would be split up in case someone was caught. You were at the museum, positioned to get a signal when the inside guys were coming out. You'd signal to Brina, and that's when she'd bring the van closer and you'd get inside and wait for Darrin."

"She told you a lot."

His voice is tight, like he can't believe that

his Sabrina would do something like that. Share those kind of secrets. Well, maybe he's right. But I still know what I know.

I offer him a tiny little smile. "You had your secrets. She had hers."

"She put us at risk talking to you."

I have to force myself not to leap to my feet. "*She* put *you* at risk? You son-of-a-bitch."

"I didn't kill her." There's ice in his voice, but I don't care. I want the truth. Maybe I won't get it out of him tonight, but I *will* get it.

Still...

I take three deep breaths, forcing myself to back off. I can't burn bridges because this man is literally my bridge to the past. I may not trust him, but I still need him. "Look," I say, keeping my voice soft and reasonable. "She told me everything. About the heist. About you. About her life on the street. It was like we were the same person, you know? That's how we were our entire life. So there was no way I would tell a soul."

I can tell he wants to argue, but then he makes a swiping motion with his hand. "Fine. Go on."

"That was pretty much it. The two teams would meet up, get the stones to a pre-arranged buyer that Tim had set up, and that was that." I grin. "How did I do?"

"A-plus," he says. "Tell me the rest."

"You tell me about the text."

"Tell me more about what my role was—not security. The part where you said I was waiting. Tell me all of that, and you can probably take a guess about the text."

I want to argue, but I want answers more. So I press on. "Sabrina was driving. You were her—what do you call it? Her wingman. And while Darrin and Tim were inside, you were supposed to just be a bystander in the alley by the service entrance, somewhere between that door and the getaway car. You wore a headset, and they signaled when they were coming out. Beeps or something."

"Why couldn't they just signal me and Brina in the van?"

"Because of the low-range frequency they had to use inside the museum. Using a higher range would have corrupted the hacks you and Brina had done to the in-place security."

He nods, looking both annoyed that I know so much, and impressed by how well I understand.

"That's why they needed an intermediary.

They couldn't signal Jorge or Brina directly. So once you signaled, you'd walk back toward the van. It was, what? About two blocks away? And you could see it, right?"

He nods. "Not consistently. Sometimes traffic blocked it. But we timed it out. I could get to the van in less than the time it took for Jorge to circle around to it."

"That's all I know," I tell him. "Except that you didn't walk back. And you never got into the van. And now you're alive. You may say you didn't play a part in blowing the woman you supposedly loved to bits, but I don't believe you. So if you want a chance to convince me, now's the time. Tell me about this text that's somehow the reason Sabrina's dead."

"I never wanted to leave her alone. I protested that point in all of our planning sessions. But the other guys—and there were only guys—insisted. And like you said, because of the short-range communications, we needed someone to relay the *ready* message."

"Keep going."

"We timed it," he said. "Ninety-seven seconds. But on that day I got a text from her."

A chill races up my spine. "From Sabrina. You got a text from Sabrina?"

"Telling me to hold off. To wait until she signaled again."

It's everything I can do not to leap the short length of the sofa and claw his face off.

"*Sabrina* texted you."

His throat moves as he swallows. "I thought so at the time. Now, though..."

I ease back. Just a little. "What do you mean?"

"She had a radio, too. No interference between the van and my position. I could hear her clear. We were on radio silence that day, but we'd run scenarios before the actual operation."

"And?"

"And she and I had decided that if we had to abort or adjust, we'd go against protocol and use the radio. The odds of someone monitoring the frequency were slim. The odds of someone digging up a text later...well, still slim, but a slightly greater risk."

"And you're saying that she texted you anyway."

"I thought she did. But now I'm certain it wasn't her. Someone spoofed her number. Someone wanted me on the sidewalk. They wanted me watching." I hear the break in his voice, but he goes on, the words heavy and shaky. "Someone wanted me to watch the van explode with the love of my life inside it."

The pain I hear in his voice is almost unbearable, and I have to steel myself against it. Of course, he feels pain. After what he did, the fires of hell are probably already burning his feet.

"You saw her? In the van, I mean. You actually saw her when it—when it happened?"

Slowly, he shakes his head. "The street was slightly angled, so I saw more of the passenger side. Plus, with the way the sun hit the windshield, I couldn't see inside the van at all."

Once again, he puts his face in his hands, and I can hear the scratch of beard stubble against his palms as he rubs, as if trying to wash away sin.

"Sometimes, I wish I had seen her in there. Maybe then it would feel real. Maybe then I could move on. But I can't. It's been fifteen years, and it feels like yesterday. Her life ended when that van exploded. And even though I'm still here—even though I go to work and have friends and pretend to have a life—the truth is that mine ended, too."

My heart should break for him. Except it doesn't. Because I don't believe him. I know too much about him. About that night. I know now that there was a plan to take out most of the team. That only a few of the players ever intended to walk away with the Sisters. And Brax was one of them.

But now the Sisters are about to be displayed again. And I happen to know there's going to be another attempt to steal them. Only this time, it will be successful.

I know, because I'm the one arranging it. I'm getting Sabrina's old team back together again. I'm going to get revenge.

And this man is going to help me.

I tilt my head to the side, biting my lower lip as I study him. "Sabrina died for nothing. The heist was botched. The Sisters never even left the building."

"You think that matters to me? She's dead. I don't give a fuck about the stones."

"I do." I scoot closer to him on the sofa. "They're about to be displayed again. Help me steal them."

He looks at me like I've lost my mind. "What the hell are you talking about?"

"Think about it. Who would know to send you a text about holding off approaching the van? Some random hacker? No way. It was someone on the team. Someone who had a reason for killing her off."

His eyes narrow. "I thought you believed that I killed her. That I'm bullshitting you about the text."

I shrug. "I do think that. But I'm willing to be proven wrong. All I want is justice for my sister."

"And stealing the Sisters will get you that?"

I smile. "If we get the same team together, then yeah. Or it'll get me closer, anyway. I've already reached out to Darrin. Turns out he already had the Sisters on his radar. Great minds, and all that. I have a meeting set."

"You want to work with him on this new heist in the hopes of figuring out what happened on the first heist? You really think that's going to help us figure out who Sabrina's real killer was?"

"I think it's better than doing nothing. And so do you."

His brows rise. "Do I?"

"You said *us*," I point out. "Help *us* figure out who her killer was." I tell myself that was an intentional move on his part, not a check in the He Didn't Do It column.

"I do want to help you. I'm just not sure that stealing the Sisters is the best way to go."

"You have a better plan?"

He grins. "No."

I lean forward more and put my hands on his knees. "Then help me, Brax. You say it wasn't you? Help me prove it. Maybe you don't care what I believe, but if you're not bullshitting me, then you do care about Sabrina. You want justice for her, right? Then help me find out what really happened."

"Steal the Sisters."

"They're going to be on display at a Performing Arts Center. I mean, come on. From what I know, that would be a cakewalk for the original team. Help me," I repeat, taking his hand and ignoring the frisson of electricity that shoots through me from nothing more than the brush of skin against skin.

He pulls his hand back, and I exhale a breath in relief. Then he stands and starts pacing. "That's not what I do anymore."

"I believe you," I say, even though I'm sure he's lying. This isn't a man who's gone straight; considering everything I know about him, I wouldn't have expected him to.

He's too good at what he does. And definitely too cold-hearted.

Once upon a time, I never would have

believed that. As far as I was concerned, he was warmth and humor, and I truly believed that he loved me. But that was before he got some text that "delayed" him.

Delayed, my ass.

Delayed is what saved his life. And as for me ... well, I'd be nothing more than ash now if I hadn't been forewarned and pulled out by agents from Group Ultra—a deep cover arm of the Sensitive Operations Command—a covert government intelligence organization that saved me and then recruited me.

They told me the truth about the man who'd supposedly loved me. They backed it up with evidence, and they gave me time to mourn. Both my "death" as I transformed into "Samantha," the twin sister who'd never really existed but who now magically has a birth certificate, and the loss of Brent, the man I'd loved, now living his life as Braxton Reed, using the next name on our list of aliases, just as I'd known he would.

Still, despite what my saviors told me, I never wanted to believe that the man who now calls himself Brax would kill the woman he loved. And that leaves one of three options:

Maybe I was just wrong, and he's always been a cold-hearted killer.

Maybe he had nothing to do with rigging the van, and it was only a coincidence that he didn't return in time for the explosion.

Or maybe he really is innocent, and there's someone else pulling the strings.

I wish I could believe the last. But when you grow up the way I did, you don't believe in fairy tales or happily ever afters. I'm going to prove what he did. And once I do, Brax will be the one in the ground. And I'll be Sabrina again. The last gal standing.

CHAPTER FIVE

C ami Green leaned back in the Fifties retro chair, then lifted her morning coffee from the blue Formica dining table. "So I guess that means I don't get to say it any more."

Brax kept his lips from twitching by taking a sip of his own coffee. "What's that?"

"That you're not the boss of me."

They shared a grin, and she raised one perfectly groomed eyebrow, her skin glowing from the habitual morning workout he'd interrupted by coming over unannounced. "Seriously," she continued. "Congrats on leading Omega team. We've got a good thing going at Stark Security."

"No regrets?"

She shook her head, tossing her long blond

ponytail. She'd just finished a three-week long undercover assignment and had taken some time for herself in Palm Springs, which had meant skipping the party at Damien Stark's house. He knew she was probably exhausted—and he knew that this could wait until Monday. Except it couldn't.

With anyone else, he would have simply waited until the next day to brief her, when she officially returned from her post-operation leave. But this was Cami, and it wasn't just about briefing her on a new op.

He needed someone to talk to. About this new assignment. About Samantha's unexpected entrance into his life. And about the overlap between those two events. And she was the only person in the world he could share all of that with.

"Why are you really here?" She asked, reading his mind as usual. She stretched one legging-clad leg out onto the other chair. "It's not just about you leading up Omega."

"Sabrina."

The fact that her eyes barely widened was testament to how good Cami was at her job. She had the kind of face that was almost entirely unreadable. But she did shift her position, putting both feet on the ground and leaning forward, her hands cupping her mug, her brown eyes laser-focused on him.

"I'm listening."

"Her sister showed up. Her identical twin."

He could tell from the expression on Cami's face that she understood just how deeply seeing Sabrina's face on another woman had cut him.

"Brax ... I'm so sorry. That's—wow. I mean, that's unexpected. Which I guess is the under-statement of the year."

"That about sums it up."

"She showed up out of nowhere? What happened? What did she say?"

He told her. Everything from getting the text to shutting the door behind her when she left his apartment last night.

"Holy shit." The word hung in the air. "How are you doing? That's such a lame fucking question, but seriously—how are you doing?"

He waved the words away. "I'm fine."

"The hell you are." She leaned forward, her elbows on the table. "Remember who you're talking to."

"I do," he said. "Why do you think I'm here?"

She hadn't taken Sabrina's place in his heart—no one could ever do that. But she'd filled a gap that had desperately needed filling. In a way, they'd saved each other when they'd bonded in the back of a van after being pulled in for "police questioning" that had turned out to be a secret government recruiting program.

"Yeah," he said. "You're right. I'm not fine. I'm ripped up all over again." He sighed and rubbed his temples. "On the one hand, I don't want this assignment. On the other, if it leads me to whoever planted that bomb, it will be worth it."

"She thinks *you* had something to do with it. Maybe even planted it. Who knows what she's got planned, but have you considered that she may not be looking for the killer. She may just be looking for revenge."

"I know."

"There's another possibility, too."

"She may not even care about revenge," he said. "She may be planning to steal the Sisters herself."

"Exactly. You don't know a thing about her, and the fact that Sabrina never told you about...."

"What?" He heard the accusation in his voice and wished he could call back the word.

She leaned back in the chair and crossed her arms. "Don't play naive. You never saw Sabrina's body. Maybe she and her sister were pulling some sort of long con. Maybe they were aiming to grab the Sisters, and it all went bad. Maybe her current plan isn't to figure out who planted that bomb. Maybe that's just a ruse to steal the stones now."

He shook his head. "No."

"Is that your heart, your head, or another part of your body talking?"

"Dammit, Cami." He realized he'd pushed back from the table and was standing. "Don't play shrink with me."

"I'm just saying out loud what you already know, even if you're not admitting it to yourself."

He paced the length of her kitchen, from the little door that opened onto her small garden, past the long counter with the sink until he paused in front of the stove. He turned the knob, then stared into the blue flame that burst out from the nearest burner.

"I have to know," he finally said. He turned off the flame and turned back to her. "And since me knowing is completely in-line with the mission, none of your questions really matter. Do they?"

He met her eyes. She held them, her chin lifted, her arms still crossed.

"I want you on my team, Cami. Not just on the op—that's Ryan's call. I need you on the inside, too. Part of the heist crew."

"Yeah, about that. What did Ryan say when you told him you were involved in the original job."

"Not a thing."

She rolled her eyes. "You have to tell him."

"No."

"Dammit, Brax. He's your boss. This job was a fucking gift, you know that. There were rules when we were recruited, and—"

"Counter-espionage rules. FBI rules. But we're not FBI anymore, and this isn't an FBI op, and we're not pulling government paychecks."

"And you think that matters? Hell, we probably owe Stark Security even more. These people have been like family, and Peterson vouched for both of us," she added, referring to their Assistant Special Agent in Charge who'd recommended them to Ryan.

"You're right," he said. "You're one-hundred

percent right. I should have told Ryan and Mason at the table. At the very least, I should tell Ryan now."

"Exactly. We can—"

"But I'm not going to. Not yet."

Her gaze didn't waver, and it wasn't until he reached *eight* that he realized he'd been counting in his head. "Cami? I need you on this."

Another three beats. Then she sighed as the hint of a smile touched her lips. "Been a long time since I helped pull off a robbery. If you want me in, then I'm in."

"Thanks." He felt a hundred pounds lighter.

"Having a best friend can be a real pain in the ass. You know that, right?"

He gave her a hard stare. "Oh, yeah. I know that."

"Ass." She punctuated the word with a smile as she stood and crossed to stand in front of him, then gently took his hand. "This sister ... she's not Sabrina."

"I know that."

"I know you *know* it. But will you remember it when it matters?"

"Of course, I will," he said. But he saw the

way her eyes narrowed. And even to his own ears, the words sounded like a lie.

Lucky B's in Panorama City is the kind of bar where the grease from all the fried food gets into your skin if you stay for more than a few hours. The kind where the locals know each other's names, but don't pay attention to outsiders.

The kind where both college kids and motorcycle gangs come to shoot pool. Where the conversation in one of the dark booths could be first-date banter or the low, whispered plan for a murder.

It's where Brax and I—well, he's back to being Brent now— have come to meet up with Darrin Gold, the man who'd been the master-mind behind that fatal—supposedly, anyway—first attempt to steal the Sisters.

We make our way across the sticky floor, and as we reach the booth, Darrin half-rises in greeting, his eyes on me, without even a glance toward Brax.

"Holy shit, Sabrina. It's really you?" He studies my face, his pale blue eyes wide as he shakes his head slowly, like a high school dropout tossed into a seminar on advanced calculus. "I can't believe it. I mean—nothing personal—but aren't you supposed to be dead?"

I shrug. "I've never been big on doing what's expected. Or on dying, for that matter."

"But how—"

"It's me," I tell Darrin, cutting him off as I release Brax's hand so that I can slide into the booth. Brax settles in beside me. Then, as we'd discussed, he puts his arm around my shoulder, and I lean into him, all the while watching Darrin's obviously shocked face.

"I don't use that name anymore," I tell him, pretending not to notice the way he's now frowning at the supposed intimacy between me and Brax. And pretending not to notice how good it feels to be back in Brax's arms.

Stop it.

With a sharp order to myself to keep my head in the game, I lock my eyes on Darrin's and keep my expression flat. "I'm sure you understand why."

"Sorry. Understand what?"

"Why I don't go by Sabrina. She's dead, isn't she?"

"I damn sure thought so." He drags his fingers through spiky dark hair streaked with gray. If someone told me to conjure a picture of a criminal, an image of Darrin would have popped into my mind.

Not surprising. After all, the guy's a conman and a thief. And an exceptional one at that. Years ago, he was quite good looking. But the face that had once been appealing is now so sallow and lined that most people probably assume he's in his sixties. He's not. He's forty-one. And as far as I'm concerned, the faded good looks are just one more drop in the Bad Karma bucket. And he deserves a full-on flood.

"I wasn't sure what to think when you called and told me who you are. But I don't think I really believed it was true until you walked through that door. Hell, I think I'm still in shock." He forces a pathetic grin. "You should probably slap me so I know I'm awake."

To his surprise—and mine—I do, rising up and leaning over the booth as my palm lashes out to intersect his cheek.

"*Careful,*" Brax whispers, but I ignore him. It felt good. *Really good.*

And why not? Haven't I been waiting months—no, years—for this opportunity, never truly believing I'd have the chance to settle the score. Darrin's the one who'd pulled me in, after all. And if Brax is telling the truth about his own innocence—a very big if—then Darrin may well be the one who wired that van.

I don't know. Not yet.

But I'm going to find out.

Around us, the other patrons have frozen. A burly man carrying a tray starts to come over. I hold up a finger and shake my head. "We're fine."

He stops in front of us, saying nothing. He's a mountain of a man with a jovial face. A fatherly sort who would undoubtedly go out of his way to protect a woman. "Really," I add. "Thanks, but I'm okay."

His eyes narrow, as he looks from Darrin to Brax and then back to Darrin again. Eventually, he nods. "You need anything," he says, talking only to me, "you just say the word."

I nod and flash my most charming smile, and when the waiter—maybe manager?— turns away, Brax leans forward.

"You should know better than to test her," he tells Darrin, his voice low and calm.

Darrin's eyes skip from me to Brax, the baffled pleasure on his face shifting to some-thing much darker. "I find it interesting that you're here at all, Brent. We all assumed you planted that bomb."

"You assumed wrong," Brax says, with a casual shrug, like we're just hanging in a bar having a conversation with an old friend.

In a way we are. If that old friend might be inclined to kill you.

"Whatever you say." Darrin punctuates the words with the scary smile I remember from back in the day. "Just odd, you know. You don't get back to the van like we rehearsed dozens of times. And then the van goes boom and you run away. Which really wasn't part of the plan." He traces his finger around the top of his beer. "You can see why we might have been confused. Especially when you didn't end up accompanying us to prison. Just a little bit of follow-the-dots logic that doesn't quite work out for me."

"That's because you followed those dots to the exact wrong conclusion." Brax says the words with a bored matter-of-fact tone, but offers no more explanations or protests.

Smart. He's avoiding the whole *he doth protest too much* problem. And as any long-time con knows, less is always more.

"You trust this guy?" Darrin asks, turning his attention back to me.

"I do," I say, even though I don't. Or, rather, I don't completely.

"Really?" The word has a dry, disbelieving tone. Under the circumstances, I can't say I blame him. "He's alive, and you're a walking corpse. And you trust him. You actually trust him."

"I already told you I do," I say, meeting his eyes and holding them. "Do I strike you as a stupid woman?"

His eyes narrow. "No."

"Then you'll have to assume that I'm not being foolish in trusting him."

I turn to Brax. And though the truth is that I absolutely do *not* trust him, I cup the back of his head, lean forward, and surprise him with a kiss. The kind that's long and slow and intimate.

The kind that I immediately realize was a huge mistake. Because I like it too damn much.

I start to pull away, but he holds me close, deepening the kiss even as his hand finds its way to my thigh. I stifle a moan, wanting nothing more in that moment than to be in the past. Fifteen years ago when I didn't know what I know now.

Or, rather, when I didn't believe what I now believe.

But this is the present, and his lips take me back to a time when he was my entire world. When I trusted him as much as I trust myself. When I knew with absolute certainty that he would never harm me.

A time when I'd been a damn little fool.

And, unfortunately, a time my body still remembers, because right then, I want nothing more than to surrender. Right here in this bar, on this bench, even in front of Darrin. I just want *him*. Brent. The man I'd loved. Not Brax, this man I no longer know.

Frustrated, I order myself to ignore the way my nipples stiffen against my bra as well as that sweet, tingling sensation between my thighs in anticipation of an even more delicious touch.

I pull away, forcing myself to meet his eyes —hoping he can see the coldness in them as I say ever so sweetly, "Careful what you start, baby. Whatever Darrin may be hoping for, you know I'm not into exhibitionism."

The corner of his mouth curves up, and his hazel eyes aren't cold at all. Instead, they're gold with flecks of green, and I see reflected in those deep, warm pools a desire as deep as my own.

Not good. Really, really not good.

Across the table, Darrin's looking at me with

interest, but despite all the classes I've taken on human psychology and how much I've practiced reading expressions, I can't read his. Perhaps he's turned on. Perhaps he's shocked that I could still want this man after what he did. Perhaps he knows perfectly well that we were faking.

Except right now, I'm not sure that Brax was faking. For that matter, I'm not sure that I was either.

Thankfully, Darrin's low chuckle grounds me again, letting me abandon that line of thinking.

I settle back into the booth and flash what I hope is a heat-filled look toward Brax and then a smug glare toward Darrin. "As I was saying, Brent's part of the team. I trust him. You should, too. And with Tim in the ground, we need him if we're going to ace this job. Something we missed by a pretty wide margin fifteen years ago."

"Go on," Darrin says.

I lift a shoulder in a casual shrug. "I've already said my piece. We're part of the team. You know that as well as we do. I assume you've already got Jorge on deck, right?"

I shoot Brax a self-congratulatory smile.

During the drive, I'd had him quiz me on the names of everyone who'd been involved the first go-round, so I wouldn't confuse Jorge with Jose again. I know the names perfectly well, of course. But I don't want to give Brax any reason to question my story. Not yet.

Eventually, of course, I'm going to reveal all and then rip the heart out of this man who'd betrayed me after swearing he loved me.

Eventually.

But not quite yet.

I return my attention to Darrin, watching as he digests the silent demand I just put on the table: either pull Brax and me into the heist he's planning or run the risk of finding out that somehow the cops learned about what's about to go down.

There's not a sound at our table for over a minute. We're like a bubble of silence surrounded by the ambient hum of a crowded bar. Then—when I'm starting to think he's gone mute—he finally speaks.

"Looks like the old gang's back together," he says. "Seems like a damn good omen to me."

"Almost the old gang," Brax says. "We had a team of five originally for a reason. Tim clearly won't be joining us."

"Guy never could hold his temper. Irritated the wrong guy. Got a shiv for his trouble." Darrin shudders, then waves his hand as if washing all that unpleasantness away. "But it's not a problem. Jorge's in for sure. As for Tim's replacement, I know a few guys. One of them should be able to handle it."

"Don't bother," Brax says, and both Darrin and I turn to him. "I've got it covered."

"Wh—," I begin, but Darrin gets there first. "Who is he?"

"She," Brax says. "We've worked together before. She's solid. And she's got incredible fingers."

Darrin's eyes narrow. "I'm not sure—"

"No, it's fine," I say, speaking more forcefully than I intended, as if to make my words that much more true. As if by agreeing so readily I can cap off the jealousy that's pressing at my ribcage like an oil well about to turn burst into a geyser.

Jealous?

No. No way. No fucking way. I'm over this man. I've been over him for years.

More important, I don't trust him.

And this man doesn't even know I'm me.

"We'll want to meet her," I add once I

realize I've let silence linger a few beats too long. "Me and Darrin and Jorge." I shoot Darrin a sideways glance that I hope conveys that he needs to keep his mouth shut. "We need to make sure she's a fit for the team. But," I continue, turning my attention from Brax to Darrin, "Brent headed up security last go-round. So he should pick his team."

While Brent and I had hacked the museum-wide security system to allow for, among other things, a full-failure of the lock-down system, Tim had been on-site in the uniform of an actual security guard while Darrin had posed as a docent.

While Brax and I had hacked the system so that we could manipulate the lock on the room and the display case, the case itself had a final lock that was off-the-grid. An accomplished thief, Tim's job was to get through that final lock.

Darrin scowls. "Last go-round didn't exactly have a stellar conclusion."

"That wasn't Tim's fault," Brax points out. "My girl is solid."

I expect Darrin to argue. The truth is, I've never known exactly what went wrong. Just that the mission fell apart. And somewhere, in the middle of all that, I died.

To my surprise, Darrin only nods. "Fine. We meet her. All of us. We give her the thumbs-up, then we're green-lit on this thing. She pushes any buttons, though, and we're going to be having a conversation."

"That sounds like a plan," Brax says. "Doesn't it baby?" He squeezes my shoulder, then pulls me close and brushes a kiss over my hair, his lips grazing my ears. I'm more pulled-together than I was a moment ago, but there's no escaping the sensual tremor that races up my spine.

"A plan," I say stupidly. "Yeah. I'll text you the meeting time and place tomorrow," I tell Darrin. I've come prepared, and now I haul the purse I'd tossed beside me on the bench seat into my lap. I take out two burner phones and pass them to Darrin, one after the other. "Yours. Jorge's." I hand another to Brax, who is looking at me with such an odd expression, I have to turn away.

"The lady came prepared," Darrin says, and I'm ridiculously grateful he's given me an excuse to talk more to him.

"Always." I smile. "And this," I add, holding

up a business card for a local coffee shop, on which I've already scribbled all of the cell numbers, four labeled with D, J, B, and S.

I look at Brax and tap the final number. "Her name?"

"Carly," he says, and I scrawl a C on each of the cards in front of her burner number. I do it in pencil. "In case we don't agree," I add, then share a smile with Darrin, as if we've just bonded like long-lost friends.

I hand Darrin and Brax their cards, then pass a second one to Darrin. "You'll get Jorge his phone?"

Darrin nods. "What about Carly? She's not in until we all say she's in."

"Then we meet tomorrow night," Brax says.

"Good," Darrin says. "We need to, anyway. The sisters will only be on display opening night. After that, they're being replaced by counterfeits."

Brax leans back, taking his arm off my shoulder and leaving me feeling oddly abandoned. "Where'd you get that intel?"

"Doesn't matter. It's solid."

"It matters," Brax says. "Opening night's in two weeks. Closing night is three weeks after that. You're taking away twenty-one days of possible planning and rehearsing. We lose twenty-one days, I want to know why."

"Fine," Darrin says. "I don't know. Intel came from Jorge. Ask him yourself tomorrow. All I know is it's solid."

Brax doesn't look happy. "I will. Believe me."

"Then I guess we both have an agenda tomorrow. Jorge's solid. I hope your girl is, too."

"She is," Brax says, and the genuine affection I hear in his voice curdles in my gut.

It's not jealousy. How could it be?

I don't want this man. Not anymore. Not after what he did to me. This attraction is nothing more than the aching remnant of a long history. A happy history that he'd ripped to shreds.

And for that, he deserves to suffer. And if he and this Carly person are an item, well, then that doesn't sound like suffering to me. So naturally, I'll be forced to hate her.

"Tomorrow, then," Brax says, sliding out of the booth and holding his hand out to help me. I almost ignore it. I don't need his help.

But everyone will expect us to be a couple. And at the end of the day, all I really want is to know why he betrayed me ... then make him pay through the nose.

And when you get right down to it, what better way to do that than to bring him close, build him up, and then bask in the metaphorical sunshine while I knock him the fuck back down?

CHAPTER SIX

"Are you sure you're going to be able to handle this?" Brax says to me once were back in the car. "Sabrina knew the drill. We had a rhythm together. She knew how to pull off a con, and she knew her way around a security system."

I shift in the passenger seat to face him. His car is a baby blue Mustang convertible, and seeing it in the street when he'd picked me up earlier had almost done me in. Now, I rub my palm on the well-tended leather seat, and try not to remember all the times I'd been inside her.

"Samantha?"

I blink, realizing I'd been looking right at

him, but not seeing him. Or, rather, seeing him from the past. Not as Braxton, but as Brent. Not owning this car, but sitting behind the wheel on the lot of a vintage dealer trying to talk himself into buying it.

"This is Old Blue, isn't it?"

For a moment he simply looks confused. Then his expression shuts down entirely and he turns away from me, his hands at ten and two, his face forward. We're parked on a dimly lit street a block from the bar we'd just left. His face is cast in shadows, so I can't tell if it's genuine grief I see play across his features or merely a trick of the light.

Perversely, I want it to be grief. But I'm not sure if that's because I want him to suffer because he tried to kill me. Or if I want some evidence that he truly cared for me so deeply that even now the wounds are raw.

I close my eyes, hating myself for refusing to fully accept what I know he did.

And yet, I can't. Some tiny part of me still wants to trust him.

What the hell is wrong with me?

I've seen the evidence. I've known since that night that he knew the van was rigged. All that talk about getting a text from me was bullshit.

Unless it wasn't.

I want to reach up and slap my own face. There's a reason Brent—*Brax*—was such a good con man. He has a way with people. He makes them like him. Makes them fall under his spell.

I thought I'd be immune, what with the whole believing he killed me thing. And yet here I am making excuses for the bastard.

Seriously. What the fuck is wrong with me?

"Hey." The word is as soft as the hand he puts on my knee. I turn to him, and I draw in a sharp breath, undone by the concern on his face. I try to tell myself it's not real—the man's a born con artist, after all—but somehow it doesn't matter. I'm so tired and it's all just piling up on me. And the way that kiss in the bar had felt really isn't helping matters.

The pathetic truth is that I want to slide into his arms. I want him to hold me the way he used to. I want him to tell me it will all be okay.

But he won't. He can't. And I hate whatever weakness in me makes me want it.

We're not allies anymore, even if it's my job to make-believe that we are. And that's something I need to keep telling myself. Over and over, for as long as it takes. *It's just make-believe.*

"I'm sorry," I say, opening the glove box and

pulling out a tissue from the small box I knew would be in there. "I'm just—all this talk of Sabrina, all these memories. I'm feeling overwhelmed."

"You two were close." He says it as a statement, not a question.

"I've already told you that."

"I know. But there's a difference between being close and, well, *being*."

I start to ask what he's talking about, but he continues before I can get a word in.

"No more Samantha," he says. "You're Sabrina now. Twenty-four/seven until this is over. We can't risk Darrin or Jorge catching a whiff of the truth."

"Do you think I don't know that?"

"How can I know one way or the other? I barely know you." His voice is tight. As if he's reminding himself of that fake truth, just like I've been reminding me.

"I guess you're just going to have to trust me when I say I haven't been sitting in a rocking chair crocheting afghans for the last fifteen years."

"Crocheting afghans?" We're at a red light, and he turns to face me, amusement dancing over that sculpted face.

"Twiddling my thumbs. Dancing naked through the daisies."

His eyes widen at the latter, and I want to kick myself. That used to by my—well, Sabrina's —favorite expression.

"Point is," I say, firmly back-peddling, "I know more than you think. And I'm a hell of a lot more like my sister than you can imagine."

I watch as his eyes slowly look me up and down. When he reaches my face, his eyes dart quickly away, as if he's afraid I'll see too much.

"I'm beginning to realize that."

Something in his tone makes my breath hitch, and for a moment, I wonder if he's had an epiphany and seen the truth.

And then I wonder if I want him to.

My entire body goes tense, but whether it's from desire or fear, I don't know. I tell myself that the only reason I want him to know it's really me is because that revelation will hurt him. And I want him to hurt.

No, not just want. I *need* to hurt him. Because he took everything from me when he betrayed me. He was the man who'd brought me back to life. Who'd taught me how to trust. How to love.

And then he'd pulled the entire damn rug out from under me.

Bastard.

"You okay?"

I draw a breath, yanked from my thoughts. "I'm fine. Why?"

He shakes his head, but doesn't answer. Instead, he says, "She told you about Old Blue."

I should simply say yes. But some perverse part of me takes over and I hear myself saying, "What are you talking about? Who told me?"

His brow furrows. "Sabrina."

I laugh. "Come on, babe. You didn't even drink that much. What kind of game are you playing?"

He'd started the car earlier, but hadn't yet put it into gear. Now, he kills the engine. "Game?"

I tilt my head and narrow my eyes. "Of course, I know Old Blue. I was with you when you bought her. Not to mention the half-a-dozen times you went to the lot before you finally talked yourself into it."

I see his Adam's apple move as he swallows. I lean back, looking casually into his eyes, only to be lashed by the pain I see there. Pain and loss so intense I wish I hadn't started this. More, it makes those doubts bubble back up again. That maybe he really is innocent. Maybe he had nothing to do with the van at all.

Maybe his pain is as real as mine.

"Sabrina?"

My name sounds like a prayer, and it takes all of my strength not to reveal everything right then.

Instead, I shift in the seat, so that I'm facing him rather than the road. "You said it yourself. If I'm going to be her, I have to be her."

His shoulders slump, as if I've just stolen all the color from his world. Right then, I wish I could call back my words. I'd wanted to hurt him—true. But that wasn't the reaction I'd expected. I'd anticipated guilt mixed with pain, not this horrific longing that breaks my heart. Not this profound sadness that makes me wonder—once again—if everything I've believed is horribly, painfully wrong.

"I'm sorry," I whisper.

He shakes his head, as if he can't manage words right then.

"I shouldn't have teased you about the car. She told me, of course. She talked about how adorable it was that you'd go back every day, wanting it so badly. You'd never had money before. Then some con had scored big, and you were flush. But you couldn't bring yourself to spend it." I know exactly what *some con* was, but I decide to be vague, afraid I'll play the part too well.

"I'm going to find out who planted that bomb," I say, both because it's true and because it feels like another way to toss my camouflage back up. "I'm going to find out who killed her."

"I hope you do. And when you do, I want five minutes in a room with them."

For a moment, silence hangs between us, and I realize I'm holding myself back from comforting him.

"I was hopelessly in love with your sister."

"You always hurt the one you love."

"That's a bullshit saying from people who don't know what love is."

I just shrug. But I have to admit — even if only to myself—that for the first time in fifteen years, I'm starting to fear that I've had it wrong all along. Not just about who killed me, but about the whole course of my life since that horrible, fateful day.

The top was down as they sped along the 405 from the Valley to Venice Beach. Brax tried to keep his eyes on the road, but he kept catching glimpses of her out of the corner of his eye. Her bare feet on the dashboard. Her fingers tapping out a beat with the classic rock playlist. The red hair she hadn't bothered to tie back whipping in the wind.

Even now, he could remember the sensation of her hair, so silky between his fingers. Most often, it was colored a basic, boring brown—the better to blend into a crowd. But there were times when she'd let it grow out, then use a wig when they were on a job. And he could still recall the sweetly erotic pleasure of her hair brushing his naked chest as she teased kisses down to his navel. And then lower still.

Stop it.

Beside him, he saw her twist in her seat. "Did you say something?"

"Nope. Just listening to the radio."

"Rolling Stones. I love *You Can't Always Get What You Want*." She flashed him that adorable—and far-too-familiar— smile. "For a while there, that song was my own personal mantra."

"Not anymore?"

She tilted her head as if studying him. "I've got pretty much all I want now. And I'm working on getting the rest of it."

"What's that?"

She laughed. "I already told you. Vengeance."

He took his eyes off the road long enough to meet hers.

"Good luck with that."

"Even if that means I'm getting you?"

"That depends on how you mean to get me." The words were out before he could call them back, and he wanted to kick his own ass. She wasn't Sabrina. He barely knew her. And the woman thought he was a killer.

Really not the best time to play flirty word games.

He kept his eyes on the road, but he knew she was still looking at him. He could practically feel the way she was studying his profile, as if the secret of his guilt or innocence was written in his pores.

After a few moments, she shifted again,

facing forward and putting her feet down before she reached over to fiddle with the CD player's knob as if it was the most natural thing to do, just like she always had. A habit that used to drive him absolutely apeshit crazy.

Now, he said nothing. How could he with the giant lump in his throat?

He knew she wasn't Sabrina. He *knew* it. Intellectually. Logically. But as for emotionally...

Well, that was a harder truth to swallow.

Just because they looked the same didn't mean they were the same. The outside of a person didn't define the person inside. He knew all of that.

And yet...

And yet with Samantha there were so many little things. Tiny jabs to his memory that were somehow both painful and wonderful. That sideways, quirky smile. The Laser of Death glare when she was pissed off. The musical lilt in her voice when she was being sarcastic, as if the sarcasm was about to lead into a Broadway musical number.

Then there was Old Blue. She *knew* this car.

And the kiss. That mind-altering, bring-a-man-to-his-knees kiss in front of Darrin.

He knew she wasn't Sabrina. And yet he couldn't *feel* that reality. It was because he didn't want to, of course. Because having Not-Sabrina in his life was a hell of a lot better than not having Sabrina.

Even if Not-Sabrina believed he'd killed her.

Fuck it.

With a sudden impulse, he cut across two lanes of traffic, and barely made the exit for Mulholland.

"Not to be picky, but my hotel's in Santa Monica. Which I'm pretty sure isn't off of Mulholland Drive."

"Big plans tonight?"

"Oh, absolutely. A wild night of partying at the No-Tell Motel." She put her feet back up on the dash and twined her fingers behind her head. "I'm just a party hound."

"I've got someplace I want to show you."

She tilted her head to look at him. "Where?"

"You'll see soon enough."

He hadn't driven Mulholland in months, and it took a while to find the scenic overlook that looked out over the San Fernando Valley.

The sun had set almost an hour ago, and the vista below them seemed like more of a starry landscape than the sky above, the actual stars dim from the ambient light and the glow of a full moon.

"This is one of my favorite places. Sabrina found it. She loved driving this road. We used to get take-out and just sit on the hood of the car and eat dinner and watch the lights below us.

"It's beautiful." Her voice was soft, almost reverential. "She—she told me about that. I tried to picture what she described."

"How'd you do?"

She turned to him, her face shining in the moonlight. "It was beautiful in my mind. But even that didn't come close." She reached out and gave his hand a little squeeze. "Thanks," she said, withdrawing her hand far too quickly.

"You're welcome."

For a moment, they just sat there, her looking out at the view. Him, looking at her.

"She used to tell me that this kind of view was why she liked driving in mountains. Because it made her feel small, just like all the people down there. Not in a bad way, but in a way that meant she was—"

"—part of something bigger," Samantha

continued. "That no matter what wrong turns she may have taken, she was still part of the whole of society. She had a place and a history. And maybe not as many people would know her history. She wasn't Queen Elizabeth or Amelia Earhart. But she was alive on earth, and that was kind of wonderful."

"*She* was wonderful."

Samantha grinned. "I won't argue with that."

"We came here before—well, the night before the heist. I brought her here. I asked her to marry me."

"No. You told her you were *going* to ask her after the heist. And you gave her your ring."

He turned to face her, frowning. "She told you that?"

"We talked all the time. I told you that."

"I just—I mean, when? We came here, we went back to the apartment to go over the plan. We—we, uh, went to bed. I was just wondering when she called you."

"It was a short call. Maybe from the bathroom? I don't know. She didn't say. But she wanted to tell me. She was excited, especially about the ring."

"It was my mother's."

"Your father killed her." The words were flat and factual, but he heard the sympathy underneath.

"He was never arrested, but yes. And the ring had been a gift from Mom's parents before the wedding. A gold band etched with a pattern of two threads intertwined. I took it off her finger at the funeral. I was only nine. I hid it, and I put it on the night I ran away."

"She didn't tell me how you got it, but she told me how much it meant to you."

"When I gave it to her up here, I told her it would be her wedding ring. I'd intended to take it back. Keep it with me until the wedding, but she wanted to wear it on her right hand, and then have me move it to her left during the ceremony."

"That's lovely."

He heard the break in her voice and looked up. He couldn't be sure in the dim light, but he thought he saw tears in her green eyes.

"Well, that's what she did. And so she was wearing it when—well, she was wearing it." He coughed, trying to mask his cracking voice. "So now I don't even have that to remember her by."

Brusquely, he brushed at his damp eyes. "You're moving into my apartment."

"Excuse me?"

"Sorry. I didn't mean for that to be an order. But the idea still stands. You're moving in with me."

She took a step backward, then perched on the hood of the car. "Why would I do that?"

"Because you're Sabrina."

Her eyes went wide. "What are you—"

"For all intents and purposes, you're Sabrina now. And someone wanted her dead. Someone believes they killed her. And that someone may be very, very irritated when they see you and believe she's alive."

"But so much time has passed. Surely not."

"I don't know," he said honestly. "The fact is, I was supposed to be in that van, too. So it's possible someone wanted me dead, too."

"And yet you're still here." She crossed her arms. "Are you actually trying to help me nail you?"

"I didn't kill her," he said. "And I think you believe me."

She said nothing. But at least she didn't deny it.

"Please," he said.

"I just don't think that's a good—"

He took a step closer. Since she was sitting on the hood of the car, there was really nowhere for her to go, so they were only inches apart. So close he could smell her shampoo.

"Listen, I know you're not Brina. But you are in danger, and I'm going to help you. She'd want me to. This isn't about grief or transference or whatever you were going to say."

Except maybe it was because he still couldn't shake the feeling that he was standing with the woman he'd loved. But he had to use his head. Had to run this op the way it needed to be run. And since he needed to protect the Sisters and she was determined to steal them, he needed to keep her close.

And, yes, he intended to keep her safe.

"Don't argue. You know I'm right."

For a moment, she looked like she was going to argue anyway. Just because he'd said not to. But then she nodded.

"Okay," she said, her voice so soft he could barely hear her. "I might as well. If I prove that you did kill my sister, at least I'll be well positioned to stab you in your sleep."

She looked up at him, the corner of her mouth curved up into a grin. "I'm not kidding."

"Tell you what. If you can prove I killed her, I'll give you the knife to do it with."

The grin turned into a full-fledged smile, and she extended her hand to shake. "All right, Brax. I think we've got a deal."

CHAPTER SEVEN

"Isn't your apartment a one bedroom?" We are at his front door, and I hear the beeps as he punches in the keypad code. The lock turns, and he pushes open the door. He pauses at the threshold and ushers me in past him. "I'll sleep on the couch," he says.

"Right." It's strange being here. I've never been to this apartment before yesterday, but even so, I know the place. How could I not? I know him so well. And even though fifteen years have passed, it's still familiar. The way he stacks his magazines so neatly on the coffee table, all the corners matching. The little framed photos that sit on the top of the small bookshelf. One, I see, is a snapshot of me.

My heart does a little flip-flop, and I walk

that direction. "When did you take this?"

The moment the words are out of my mouth, I regret them. It took me a moment, but I remember now, and I don't want to think about that day.

It's too late to call back the question, though, and I feel the tightening in my chest when I notice the way he fiddles with the ouroboros ring before answering.

"We'd gone to the beach," he says, his voice low and a little gruff. "It was a crazy day. We were just planning on walking, maybe wading in the water. We met an older gentleman who was taking his boat to Catalina. He invited us along."

He looks at me and shrugs, as if I'd asked a question. "It's not something we would've normally done, but the guy seemed nice enough. He said that he used to take his kids. Apparently they were about the same age as we were back then. So we went with him to the marina, got on the boat with him and headed to the island."

His voice is a combination of pain and happiness, a feeling I share so deeply I'm having trouble breathing. I want him to stop talking, afraid I'm going to say something to give myself away, and yet at the same time, I want this moment. I want to go into the past like this with him, as if that will somehow prove that those years together meant something to him. That we weren't—as I sometimes fear on long, sleepless nights—doomed from the beginning, only I'd been too stupid to see it.

For a moment, the melancholy fades from his face, replaced by a bright smile. "When he wasn't listening, we both told each other how crazy this was. For all we knew, he was going to shoot us and dump us in the ocean. But at the same time, considering the life we were leading, was it really that big a risk?"

"I could see Sabrina doing something like that." I remember that day so vividly. I want to tell him how much fun I had. How close I'd felt to him. So many of our days were wrapped up in lies. Not between each other—at least I never thought so—but the remnants of the cons that we were constantly pulling just to stay alive.

That day had been just us. The man, Mr. Baker, wasn't someone we were trying to get anything from. He was a little miracle that had popped up in a life that we hadn't chosen, but had made our own. And I'm actually jealous that Brax has a copy of that photo, but I don't.

"Anyway, we got to the island, and he bought us lunch at this Mexican restaurant, and then he told us to enjoy ourselves on or off the boat while he went diving. So we played on the beach. We explored the little town. And I took her picture. It was just a one-off. But it ended up being one of my favorites."

"You don't mind having it out like this? Seeing it every day."

"At first, yeah. After she—after she died, I had to put it away. I'd pass by it every day, and whatever energy I'd had for getting out the door would rush out of me. All I wanted to do was sit on the couch and stare at that photo and wish her back."

My heart twists, and I realize I want to take his hand and comfort him. That I believe him. About the pain, anyway. But that doesn't mean he's innocent. I know he loved me. But I still don't know if he killed me.

"I put it in a drawer," he continues. "But it was never really out of the way. That picture's always been in my mind. I have volumes and volumes of photo albums in my mind full of Sabrina. And I didn't like the fact that just because I was heartbroken, I was erasing her from my life. So I pulled it out of the drawer and

I put it back. Now it makes me smile. Not because she's not around, but because of the good times we had when she was."

I nod, but I don't answer. I can't. My throat is too full of tears. I take a seat on the sofa, and he perches on the coffee table in front of me.

"Listen, I have a confession to make."

I go completely cold, and I realize in that moment that I'd exonerated him in my mind. "What?" I whisper, not wanting to hear the truth, but knowing I have to.

"I know it's horrible of me, but I feel strange about the fact that she talked to you so often. Hell, I hate that you even exist, but I didn't even know about it. I thought we'd shared our lives, but there was a whole huge chunk that she completely left out." He draws in a breath, then stands up and turns away from me. "Oh, hell. I'm angry at her for keeping the truth of you from me, and I know that isn't fair, but that's the way I feel."

He turns and faces me again, and I see the truth of what he's saying in his eyes. The hurt and the pain. That feeling of betrayal.

Some part of me wants to tell him the truth. That I didn't betray him. But that's the part that believes he would never have hurt me. It's a big part, and it seems to be growing with every minute I spend with him. But there's still that basic, underlying fact. *I was in the van, and he wasn't.*

And there's more, too. Bits and pieces that add up to the near certainty that he killed me. It's almost unfathomable, and yet I know the evidence is there. What I don't understand is why he would do it.

I can't believe that I was so mistaken about our relationship. So why would he want me dead? Was it self-preservation? Had someone threatened him? Was it money?

I don't know. But I am determined to find out.

"Where did you go?"

I shake my head. "Sorry. It's just that I miss her too."

He nods, then looks away. He's turned his head so that I can't see him well, but he hasn't turned enough to hide the fact that he's wiping his eyes with the side of his finger.

When he faces me again, he tells me that he's going to go put my stuff in the bedroom. On the way here, he'd suggested we get my stuff from my hotel, and my matching rolling bag and tote are sitting by the front door.

When he comes back, he gestures towards the kitchen. "Do you want a drink? Unless you're tired and want to go to bed now."

"No, a drink would be great. Do you have a Merlot?"

"You two really were identical twins. That was her drink too, at least when she didn't have gin."

"I like gin," I say, kicking myself for almost saying *I still like gin*. "Whichever is easier."

He waves me toward the couch, and I take a seat. The kitchen is in front of me behind a breakfast bar, and I can see everything except the refrigerator and, I assume, a pantry somewhere. I hear the fridge open and see the dim kitchen brighten as it does. The light fades, and a moment later he's back at the couch with a bottle and two glasses.

He uncorks it and pours, then hands me my glass. I expect him to sit on the sofa next to me, but instead he sits on the coffee table so that our knees are almost touching. He leans forward, and I almost wish I could ease back and disappear into the cushions.

It's not that I want distance from him, it's the fact that I *don't* want the distance. That I want him to keep leaning forward until he has

to put his hands on my knees to balance himself.
I want to feel his touch again. And I am more
than a little afraid that I've overestimated my
ability to pull off this con.

"Can I ask you something?"

My stomach clinches, but I nod. I tense in
anticipation of him asking if I'm really Sabrina.
I'm certain I must have screwed up somehow.
How could I not? He clearly knows me so well.
Just as I know how smart this man is. How
clever. How quick to see beneath a con.

But that's not what he asks. Instead, he says,
"Why weren't you two traveling together?"

"What do you mean?" I know exactly what
he means.

"You two were clearly close. Like ridiculously close. And from what I can tell, you know
your way around a con. So I'm guessing that was
in your repertoire before you left home, just like
it was in hers. So why didn't you leave together?
Work together. I can think of a dozen cons that
would go brilliantly with identical twins."

I almost laugh at that. Instead, I ask him,
"What do you know about why Sabrina left
home?"

Of course, I already know the answer to
this. I'm the one who told him, after all. But

Samantha doesn't know what he knows. And besides, I want to watch his face as he tells me my own history.

He does, repeating to me the story and details I'd told him over the years. About the abuse I—well, Sabrina—suffered at the hand of my father. About the way he would beat her. Hurt her. Rape her. And then how he would use me as part of his schemes and cons, often trading me to anyone for any purpose if it would get him positioned so he could pull off a job.

When he pauses in the story, I nod, feeling tense. I shouldn't have asked. Those are years I've tried desperately to forget. "All that's true," I say, shocked my voice sounds normal.

"I'm guessing he did the same to you," Brax says.

I nod.

"Sabrina told me about the night she left. How did it really happen?"

I swallow, wishing I could tell him that I never kept anything from him. But I have to keep up the pretense.

I have to, because otherwise I'll never learn the truth.

I draw a breath. "One day he went too far. He was beating me with a whip, and I was in so much pain I was about to pass out. He finally let up and then he went and drank himself into oblivion. That's when Sabrina said she was going to end it. That she was going to kill him. And she did. She took care of it for both of us."

"And you?"

"I didn't have the stomach for it. But I watched. And I helped her clean up, of course, and then we ran. We watched the news for weeks after. And that's how we learned that the police were looking for us. For twins." I shrug. "We knew people would expect us to stick together. So we decided we had to split up."

"That must have been incredibly hard," he says.

"I think it was the hardest thing I ever had to do." The words are true, but I'm not thinking about my fake twin. I'm thinking about him. Because the hardest thing I've ever done was walking away from him. Even though I believed he'd tried to kill me, leaving just about killed me.

I keep my voice level as I continue with the story. "It was hard, but we stayed in touch. We had a protocol."

"What protocol?"

"We would switch out our burner phones every two weeks at a minimum. And we would call each other every Wednesday and Saturday at least."

"So you would share the burner phone number in the conversation before you tossed previous one?"

"We tried, but that was a little complicated. So we built a website."

"What?"

I shrug. "We built a shady little website in basic HTML." I'm desperately trying to remember what the internet was like when I ran. "Anyway, we'd go onto the site and leave each other our burner numbers whenever we changed."

"This I've got to see. What's the URL?"

I shake my head, "It's long gone. We used the New York Times classifieds as a backup. We'd check every week, to make sure one of us hadn't left a message for the other."

"None of this surprises me," he says.

"No?"

"Sabrina was one of the cleverest women I've ever known. I imagine you are, too. It was a good plan you two put together."

I am uncomfortably pleased by the fact that he's just given me that kind of praise. Since I don't know what to say, I continue with my story. "We planned out our aliases beforehand. Samantha's not my real name."

"And Sabrina wasn't hers. I know. It was Stacy."

I nod. And then without thinking about it, I add, "After you two met, that seemed like all she talked about on our calls. I thought she was an idiot for falling so hard but she swore you were perfection on a stick."

"I thought the same about her."

"I guess I was right, though. About the idiot part." I look at him hard, watching every tiny movement in his face.

"I didn't kill her."

I see nothing to suggest that he's lying, and I know—or I used to know—all of his tells. So does that mean he's telling the truth? Or that he's a more experienced con?

"You said you talked to her before the heist. But it was on a Tuesday. Didn't you talk on Wednesdays?"

"Usually. But we'd text a code if we needed to talk off the regular schedule. She did, and so I called. She told me everything. She said her share would be huge and you guys were going to leave the country and get married. That you were probably going to be gone for a long time, and you were going to be living legit. She said you might stay abroad forever."

Once again, I watch his face. He's nodding slowly and his eyes are glistening. I look away, not wanting to feel sympathy for him, but at the same time wanting everything I think I know to be wrong.

I don't want him to have killed me. I want the man I loved. I want to be able to tell him it's me.

But I'm also not willing to be stupid about it. I have to know the truth before he learns that I've been lying.

"She told me she wanted to go to France."

He nods. "I wanted the UK. English. But she said France would be an adventure, and we'd learn the language. I said her adventure sounded more like a pain in the ass." A hint of a smile touches his lips. "It wasn't a fight, but I think it was our first moment of adult compromise."

"What did you decide?"

"London. But frequent trips to France. And classes in French. And once we were both reasonably fluent, we'd move." He smiles at the memory. "Actually, that was our first real argument, too. And it was stupid, really. If she hadn't

come up with the London-then-Paris plan, I
would have eventually caved. I just wanted her.
Hell, I'd have agreed to live in the Sahara so
long as she was with me.

Every word is heavy with grief, and though I
try to hold tight to my anger, I have to admit that
I believe him. Or, at least, I want to believe him.

"I still think it's so weird that she never told
me about you," he says. " We told each other
everything."

"No, you didn't."

He swipes his hand, indicating me. "Yeah. I
realize that now."

"I mean there was other stuff."

His brow furrows. "What other stuff?"

"Honestly, I only know of one thing."

"What?"

"The threat."

He looks at me, his expression entirely
blank.

"When we talked before the heist, that's
what she said. That someone told her that you
couldn't be trusted." I watch his face, looking for
any clue. "That you'd rigged the van to explode.
That you wanted her dead."

He bursts to his feet, and I can practically
see the fury coming off him in waves.

"Who?" he demands. "Who the fuck said that?"

He runs his fingers through his hair, apparently not realizing that I haven't answered. "Someone knew," he says softly, almost to himself. "Someone knew the van was going to explode." He glances at me. "Whoever that was has to be the person who planted the bomb."

He moves to the center of the room and starts to pace, cursing under his breath, mumbling to himself. Finally, he stops and turns back to face me. "She knew there was a threat. So why would she stay in the car?"

"I guess it's because she didn't believe you'd ever do that."

"Well, she was right. I wouldn't. I didn't."

"But someone did," I say.

He seems to collapse like liquid into a puddle on the ground. He's sitting on his knees, his head bent forward. "Oh, God. Oh God, oh God, oh God."

I watch his shoulders shaking as he silently cries, and when he looks up at me, his eyes are swollen, his cheeks wet.

"She died," he says, his voice heavy with grief. "She died and her last thought was that I'm the one who killed her."

CHAPTER EIGHT

"No, no," I say, kneeling in front of him and putting my hand on his thigh. "Brax, look at me."

He lifts his head, his expression more miserable than I have ever seen it.

"She would never have believed that. Not ever." The words seem to hang in the air. I'm telling him the truth—I *didn't* believe it. Not until I was safely out of the van.

Not until after the van exploded, and I was alive despite myself. And when they showed me the proof, I became certain that my guardian angels had been right. The man I loved had tried to kill me.

But that's not what I tell him now. Instead I

tell him a lie that I wish were true. "She wouldn't believe it," I stress. "Not even if there was proof. She would have known it was fake somehow."

He looks up at me, his expression so lost that I have to fight the urge to kiss him. "She wouldn't have had time to think about it, anyway. Even if she did, it wouldn't be to blame you. She'd think that someone set her up. Not you. Someone else."

Some of the misery fades from his face. "Are you sure?"

"I know her better than anyone." I don't know what possesses me to do it, but I cup his cheek in my palm and meet his eyes. "Anyone except maybe you. Trust me."

The words linger between us, bittersweet. Because right now, in this moment, I truly believe them.

But on that day—and for the last fifteen years—I trusted my saviors—now my employers —to know who planted that bomb.

Except what if they were only right about the *fact* of the bomb? What if they got the perpetrator completely wrong?

Oh, god.

Could I have really got it so wrong? For that matter, could *they* really have been so wrong?

Surely they didn't—

I squeeze my eyes shut tight, forcing the thought to stay away. There's no way. No way they would do that.

Really? The voice in my head is harsh. *Because believing Brent fucked you over wasn't just your invitation into Group Ultra, it was the reason you walked through the goddamn front door.*

I swallow, suddenly unsure of everything.

"Hey." He puts his hand on my shoulder. "Are you okay?"

I nod, then look up at him from where I'm now kneeling in front of him. I start to rise, then slam myself back down when I realize that my goal is a kiss.

Hurriedly, I scoot backward, then slam my spine against the coffee table. I stumble to my feet, wipe my sweaty palms on my clothes, and scurry sideways so that I'm not trapped between him and the table. "I—I'm just really, really tired."

"I hear you."

I bend over and grab my wine off the coffee

table. Thankfully, I didn't slam the table so hard that it spilled, and I still have half a glass left.

I down it in one gulp.

"You should get some sleep," he says, rising. "I changed the sheets this morning. Just let me grab a blanket from the closet in there."

"I don't want to kick you out of your bedroom."

He's right beside me as I say that. He pauses, and I can see the direction his mind has gone. Why not? Mine's gone there, too. The man may well have killed me, and yet even the suggestion of him in my bed makes my insides go fluttery.

"It'll just take a second."

He heads into the room, returning moments later with a blanket. "Brax, I—" I cut myself off, unsure. I want to tell him the truth. For that matter, I want to tell him to come with me to the bed. But that's just lust talking, and I'm smarter than that. "Just—just, thank you."

"Careful," he says. "Your skills aren't as sharp as your sister's."

"What do you mean?"

He turns one hand over, revealing his palm. "If I didn't kill her, I brought you here to keep you safe." He shows me the other palm. "If I did kill her, I brought you here to keep you close."

I frown, not sure where he's going with this, but not much liking the trajectory.

"So which are you thanking me for?"

I say nothing. I know the answer I want, but I don't know if it's right.

So I don't answer at all. Instead, I say, "I can see why she loved you."

For a moment, we just look at each other. Then I take the initiative, cross the living area, brush past him, and enter the bedroom.

I turn. And then, with one last look at him, I shut the door.

In a movie, it would have been a dramatic exit. In my real life, it's anticlimactic, because I still need the bathroom. Thankfully, he's left a robe on the bed, which means I don't have to paw through my bags he'd dropped in here earlier.

Instead, I go ahead and strip down so that I don't have to carry my clothes back after my shower. Then, wrapped up in a robe that smells like him, I leave the bedroom and hurry into the hall. I don't see him, and assume he's in the kitchen or has stepped out onto the balcony.

I take a quick shower and wash my hair,

using one of his towels to pile it onto my head. I'd brought my toiletry kit with me, and after debating, I leave it hanging behind the bathroom door. Then I slide back into his robe and open the door, releasing the steam that has built up in the tiny room.

I step out and pause, my eyes closed as I enjoy the cool air against my overheated skin. When I open my eyes, I see Brax. He's on the sofa now, only a few yards away from me. He's changed into jogging shorts, and he's reading a book.

Except he's not reading. Not now, anyway. Instead, he's looking at me. I flash him a little smile. "I needed that shower. Great water pressure."

Seriously? That's *my idea of conversation?*

"Best thing about this dinky little apartment."

I glance around, then shrug. "Yeah. I see that."

We share a smile, and I'm hyper-aware of my body under the robe. Of the fact that I'm standing there, essentially naked, only a few feet from him.

He clears his throat. "I was thinking about watching a movie. But we probably shouldn't," he adds before I have a chance to jump all over that suggestion. "We have a long day tomorrow, and we're starting early."

I nod, disappointed. But he's right. He'd mentioned on the drive home that he has to pop into his office. Apparently he works at a data-entry company. "I have enough saved from the various jobs Sabrina and I pulled to only need to work part time," he told me. "And now that I'm a grown-up, insurance is important."

I'd told him that I'd made plans to meet a friend for breakfast. "A girl I almost conned back on the East Coast, but ended up being friends with. She thinks I'm a marketing consul-tant. Turns out she's on vacation here," I'd added.

All of that is a lie, of course. But I can hardly tell him I have to get to work.

"So no movie," I say, sliding my hands into the pockets of his robe.

He cocks his head as he looks at me. "Do you want to?"

I know he's talking about the movie, but my mind has gone someplace else entirely. He intended that, I'm sure. I'd heard the hint of invitation in his voice. And I know better than anyone that look of desire in his eyes.

But is it really desire? Or is he playing me? Working a con to get closer to Samantha. Trying to make sure she's being upfront with him. Playing games so he can nail down exactly what she wants from him.

The possibility doesn't sit well with me at all. I'm the one who pulls the cons, not the one who gets sucked in.

So I just shake my head and tell him I'm tired. Then I head to his bedroom and shut the door without giving him any chance to respond.

But moments later, as I'm curled up in his bed, I can't stop my racing thoughts anymore than I can control the way my body still craves him.

What if he's telling the truth?

What if he never tried to hurt you at all?

I close my eyes, blocking out the words my alter ego is whispering into my ear. Because if she's right—if nothing was ever what it seemed between us—then my entire life for the last fifteen years has been a lie.

And that's not something I'm prepared to believe.

Brax groaned as he sat up on the sofa, shirtless, but still wearing his jeans. He frowned, wondering what had awakened him. Then he heard the final beep of the keypad lock, and realized that someone was entering his apartment.

He wasn't surprised when seconds later Cami poked her head in. She was the only one other than his landlord—and the locked drawer of the personnel file at Stark Security—who knew the code.

"Toss me your shirt, will you?"

He blinked at her, still not awake enough for that sentence to make sense. She shook her head in mock exasperation and came toward him, then pulled the T-shirt he'd worn yesterday off the coffee table. She turned around so her back was to him, pulled off her tank top, then slid his shirt over her bra.

When she faced him again, she shrugged. "I spilled coffee all over myself in the car. Guy in front of me slammed on his brakes for no reason. Idiot." She looked him over. "Speaking of, I'm guessing you haven't started a pot."

"You guessed right."

He needn't have said anything. She was

already on her way to his kitchen to remedy that little problem.

He sat up, stretched, then dragged his fingers through his hair.

"You look like hell," Cami said, calling to him from over the breakfast bar.

"Great to see you, too."

"You fall asleep watching a movie again?"

"Just didn't sleep well. I'll be fine." He shoved the blanket the rest of the way off him, then got up and went to the kitchen. She already had the coffee brewing and had pulled a carton of eggs out of the fridge.

"Out," she said, shooing him away. She pointed to the breakfast bar. "Sit and talk and let me do this. Otherwise I'm just stealing your food. This way, it's payment."

"You are a marvel of rationalizations. But I'm not going to argue because that means you can deliver me a coffee."

"You got it." She grabbed his favorite mug out of the cabinet, filled it almost to the brim, then slid it in front of him. He took a sip, hoping it would bring him back to life. Honestly, Cami had it right. He should have put in a movie. That at least would have distracted him. Instead, he'd lain there on the sofa trying to sleep, but instead thinking about the woman in the bedroom.

No, not the woman in the bedroom. *Sabrina*. He'd been thinking about Sabrina.

Hadn't he?

He took another sip of coffee, then another, feeling suddenly off-balance. Sabrina had been the love of his life, and yet it wasn't her he'd been thinking about last night. It had been Samantha. The woman in his robe. In his bed.

He groaned and rubbed the bridge of his nose. Was that it? Proximity and circumstance? Was he projecting his memories of Brina onto her sister? Or was he actually attracted to the woman who was just a few yards away behind the closed door?

"You okay?" Cami stood in front of him with the coffee pot. He glanced down, and realized that somehow he'd drained the entire mug.

He passed it to her, and she frowned as she poured. "Wanna talk about it?"

He shook his head.

"Fine. Then I'll tell you what Gimble did this morning." Gimble was her pet hamster, and from the way she told the story, Gimble had decided to try out a career as an escape artist. "I mean, I have no idea how he got out of the cage. But then to get out of the habitrail ball, too...."

She shook her head, laughing. "I had to crawl all over the floor to find him, and when I did, do you know what finally urged him out from under the sofa?"

"Chips Ahoy." A reasonable guess, since that was Cami's favorite snack.

"Singing," she said. "I made up a bullshit *come out hamster* song and sang it to the tune of *Singing in the Rain*. And it worked."

She sang a bar of it, and they both cracked up, agreeing that Gimble was clearly deaf because that sound should rightfully have sent him running in the opposite direction.

"Oh, hey!" Cami said, shifting gears. "Coffee?"

It took Brax a second to catch up, and when he did, he twisted on the barstool and saw Samantha standing there in jeans and a plain white T-shirt. Her tousled hair caught the sunlight streaming in through the thin curtains, making her face seem to glow. She wore no shoes and no make-up. And as far as Brax was concerned, she was the loveliest thing he'd ever woken up to.

"Coffee?" he repeated. "Ca—Carly makes a decent pot."

"Um, sure."

He tapped the stool beside him, gesturing for her to come sit. She came, but she stood beside it, her attention on Cami who was pouring coffee. "I'm making scrambled eggs, too. Want some?"

"I—sure."

Brax frowned, wondering about the way that Samantha was watching Cami. And then he remembered the shirt and mentally groaned. Surely she didn't think...

"Carly spilled coffee all over her tank top on the way over here," he said. "She makes a great breakfast, but braking isn't one of her better skills."

"Careful, or you won't even get breakfast," Cami said, then shifted her attention to Samantha. "It's not exactly a fashion statement, but it was on his coffee table, so I commandeered it."

"Better than wearing coffee," Samantha said, sliding onto the stool beside Brax.

He'd been right. It was the shirt. But as for what that meant, he really didn't know.

They all chatted for a while as Cami made breakfast, refusing any help from either of them.

Then she slid two plates in front of them and kept her own on the kitchen counter, standing and eating while they kept talking.

"I'm really sorry about your sister," Cami said when the conversation lulled.

A sad little smile touched Samantha's lips. "Thanks. I appreciate that."

"Would it be crass to say I'm looking forward to this job?"

Samantha shrugged. "I'm just glad Brax knew and trusted you. We need a fifth."

Cami nodded. "Brax told me what happened before. How the job went bad. Sabrina. Tim getting killed in prison."

"I'm surprised you signed on," Samantha said. "When I hear you say it like that, it sounds like the Sisters are cursed."

"They probably are," Brax said. "That's what they say about the Hope Diamond. And they were cut from the same stone, after all."

"We'll be sure to bring garlic," Cami said, making both him and Samantha laugh.

"How do you two know each other?" Samantha asked. "And these eggs are amazing."

"Add pancake mix when you stir them up," Cami said. "Easiest trick in the book. And we met not long after Sabrina died. We both ended up in this community program. I guess you could say it was for lost souls, right?"

He nodded. "We helped each other out. Ended up as friends."

"I'm glad he had you," Samantha said to Cami.

Brax chuckled. "Well, that's an improvement. Yesterday, she wanted me dead. More accurately, she wanted to be the one who killed me."

Samantha aimed a sugary-sweet smile at him. "What makes you think I don't still? We just have a job to do first."

"About that," Cami said, "do you two want to fill me in—"

"Brax can." Samantha slid off the stool. "I have a couple of errands to run this morning.

He turned to her. "I can drive you wherever you need to go."

She waved away the words. "It's fine. I've got a rental back at the motel. I'll take a ride share."

He almost argued, but realized there was no legitimate reason to ask her to wait for him. None other than that he just wanted her there. True, he'd asked her to stay at the apartment to make sure she was safe, but since there hadn't been an actual threat to either of them, he could hardly demand she let him be her bodyguard.

"I'll send the texts in a bit," she said. "But we still need to decide time and place. *Oh!* Hang on." She hurried to the bedroom, then came back with the burner for Cami. "So when and where?"

"The Santa Monica Pier?" Cami suggested. "A weekday in the fall. Shouldn't be too crowded, and we can always walk down to the water if there are too many ears around."

"Meet at seven?" he suggested. "That's right around dusk."

Samantha grinned. "I do love blending into the shadows."

"Good," he said. "You'll send the texts? Hopefully Darrin got the phone to Jorge."

"I'll send from my Rideshare." She glanced at her phone. "It's ten minutes away. I need to go do my make-up." She slid her phone into her back pocket and hurried into the bathroom. Cami took a long sip of coffee, her eyes on Brax. He could practically see her brain spinning with questions.

As soon as Samantha had finished her make-up, said her goodbyes and disappeared out the door, he was proved right.

"So how much does she look like Sabrina?"

"Too much," he admitted. "There's a reason they call them identical twins."

"I figured."

"Figured?"

"You look at her like—"

"Like what?"

She shrugged. "Well, like I've never seen you look at anyone." She came around and settled onto Samantha's abandoned stool. "How are you holding up?"

"Honestly?"

"No, tell me a bullshit story."

"I'm doing just fine."

They both laughed at that.

"I almost—" He shook his head, cutting off the words.

"What?"

He started to tell her never mind, but he also knew her well enough to know she'd never let it go. "I almost came onto her last night." God knew he'd wanted to.

Cami leaned back, her arms crossed as she studied his face. "Really? Well, she's sharp and doesn't take shit and she's easy on the eyes. On that alone, she ticks your boxes. Gonna go for it?"

"Don't even play that game with me. She's Sabrina's sister. We're working together. Not just any old work. We're trying to figure out who killed Sabrina. Her twin sister. The woman I loved more than life itself. But from her perspective, I'm at the top of the suspect list"

Cami took a long sip of coffee. "Well, it's obvious what's going on."

"What?"

She faced him straight on, her expression totally deadpan. "It's been ages since you've been properly laid."

"Fifteen years," he said.

She rolled her eyes and flipped him the bird. The last time they'd slept together had been eleven years ago.

"You walked right into that," he said.

"I do love you. I just don't love you. Some-times I wish I did."

"Me, too," he admitted. "I don't know if I'll ever love anyone again."

"Brax." Her voice was gentler than he'd heard from her in years. "Don't think like that."

He shook his head. "No, I'm alright. I'm not feeling sorry for myself. I just—It's just that she was everything. But I'm luckier than most people. We crammed a lifetime into six years."

"You deserve more."

"I don't disagree. But, alas, I never learned how to turn back time."

"And yet Sam is right here."

"She's not a substitute for Sabrina."

Cami put her hand on top of his. "I know that. But maybe she's solace. A way to smooth those rough edges. Hell, maybe it will grow into more."

"In case you forgot, she thinks I killed her sister."

"Maybe she did. Now that she's hung out with you, she's probably having doubts. Especially since she's attracted to you, too."

"Bullshit."

Cami laughed. "I saw the way she looked at me when she realized I was wearing your shirt. Before she got the coffee explanation. It's a wonder she didn't pierce one of my organs with all the daggers she was shooting at me. She may not trust you, but she's attracted to you." She shrugged. "And, not to sound mercenary, but you don't know her full story. It might not be a bad idea to reel her in a little."

"What the hell, Cam?"

"Oh, please. Don't you're act all shocked. You know as well as I do that she's less of a threat if you fuck her. Unless she's a stone-cold bitch, she'll have some attachment."

He patted her knee. "Got news for you, babe: *you're* the stone cold bitch."

Her smile was pure sugar. "Why thank you darling. I always knew you saw the real me."

He couldn't help it. He burst out laughing.

She glanced at her watch. "We need to go."

"Go? Where?"

"We're meeting Ryan at the data center."

"You didn't..."

She lifted a shoulder in a half-shrug. "All I said was that we had a few things to tell him." She held his gaze. "You know we have to."

"I'm putting in a request for a new best friend."

"It'll never go through. You only qualify for the dregs."

He sighed. "All right, Mom. Let's go meet Dad so I can confess my sins and accept my penance. But if he fires me, you're gonna feel pretty damn stupid."

"I'll take my chances. And don't worry. He already knew you were a notorious con artist with zero morals before he hired you. All you're doing today is shoring up that opinion."

"Remind me again why we're friends."

"Because I'm the only one who tells it like it is."

"True," he said, but he wondered if it really was. Sabrina had never pulled her punches either. And while she was now gone, Samantha was right here. And he had a feeling that she never shied away from a hard truth, either.

CHAPTER NINE

Z-Tech Data Processing—the company that officially employed both Brax and Cami—was located two blocks from the Santa Monica offices of Stark Security. The company provided a variety of tech-based services to a multitude of businesses all around the globe. It had over three hundred employees, most of whom were exactly what they appeared to be.

Brax and Cami were not among that group.

To the other employees, they were simply workers with a security clearance high enough to allow them to do jobs for government clients in the back rooms where information that had to be isolated could be handled.

And while they both often utilized those secure workstations for their actual jobs, more often than not they weren't actually in the building, even though they entered through the front doors and no one saw them leave.

Instead, they were at Stark Security, having moved between the two buildings via the underground tunnel that, per city plans, was nothing but an alternative utility route.

At Stark Security, they were both known for what they were—agents who worked exclusively on deep cover assignments and who entered through a secure basement room to which only the most high-level agents had access. If they met outside the office, Cami and Brax were simply Z-Tech employees who the SSA employee had met while getting coffee, or through some other equally mundane route.

The whole thing was a pain, Brax thought, but it was necessary. And at the end of the day, the system protected him and Cami and the integrity of the SSA as a whole.

As for Z-Tech itself, if anyone got suspicious and investigated, they'd find that it was a subsidiary of a subsidiary of a subsidiary of Stark International. Just a corporation like any other. And a profitable one at that.

Today, he and Cami had made the underground walk from Z-Tech to the SSA, then taken the stairs up to the Intake Office, cut through the covert reception area, then entered the main office of the SSA through the kitchen.

Brax signaled to Mason to join them, then waved at Denny, Mason's wife. She grinned back, her fingers never slowing on the computer keys.

"She's chasing money," Mason said. "An embezzlement investigation. Apparently, the asshole CEO's done a pretty good job of hiding the dollars he's skimming. Too bad for him, my wife is a badass on a computer."

"That she is," Cami said.

A few other agents waved to them, but most were so engrossed in whatever they were doing that they barely looked up. Only Trevor came over, walking with them as they approached Ryan's office. "I was going to text you," Trevor said, "but since you're here. Dinner a week from Saturday? We finally finished the remodel. Ollie wants you two at our first gathering. This one's already said yes for him and Denny," Trevor added, pointing to Mason.

"I'd love it," Brax said. "But it's going to depend on this job. Plus —"

"He'd want to bring a date," Cami broke in.

Trevor's brows rose. "This have anything to do with that text you got? The sister?"

"You're a smart man," Cami said, as Brax rolled his eyes.

Trevor grinned. "Bring her along. The more the merrier. You seeing anyone?" he asked, turning to Cami.

"That would be a no."

"We could try to work on that..." Trevor let the sentence hang.

"I can manage on my own. But thanks for the invite. If we're clear the night, I'm totally in."

"We'll cross our fingers," he said, then eased back as Cami and Brax reached the door to Ryan's office.

The office was glass, but today the shades were down. Brax tapped lightly, and entered as soon as he heard Ryan's sharp, "Come in."

The three of them entered, then took seats around the small table Ryan used for meetings when the conference room seemed like overkill.

"So where are we?" Ryan asked, moving from behind his desk to join them at the table.

Mason went first, going over who from SSA he'd put on the team that would provide uniformed security for the event. "We're working with in-house security, and we've engaged an outside team as well to ensure we have good coverage and a solid person-to-agent ratio."

"Excellent. And you?" Ryan nodded to Brax.

"Everything's falling in place. We've confirmed the rumors that a heist is being planned, and we're set to infiltrate that group."

Ryan's brow rose. "Good work."

"No shit,"Mason said. "How the hell did you manage —"

"I'll get to that. In the meantime, can we get security schematics for the Center? Having that intel will up our stock considerably." He looked between Ryan and Mason.

"I'll take care of it, Ryan said. "Exact? Or do you want intentional misdirections built in?"

Brax shot a sideways glance to Cami, who lifted her hands. "You're the one who knows these people."

Right away, Brax could tell she wanted to slap her own face. He didn't blame her. But she hadn't revealed anything he hadn't intended to reveal. She'd just gotten there a little quicker than planned.

"Exact," Brax told Ryan about the specs.

"Cami and I will be safer that way." He looked between Ryan and Mason. "The intel was right. The original team that tried to steal the Sisters has regrouped. One of them died in prison, so Cami is filling that role."

"And one of them died in the van explosion," Mason said, and there's another one who's missing.

"That's only half true. In fact, the woman who died had an identical twin sister. She's agreed to stand in as Sabrina. She's going with the story that she received a tip and was able to exit the van before the bomb exploded."

He looked between the men. Ryan's face was unreadable. Mason looked impressed. Underneath the table, Cami squeezed his hand. He appreciated the support, especially since he was about to cop to the part of his life that just might get him fired. Or jailed.

"And the fifth man?" Mason asked. "The one they never found? Did you manage to infiltrate yourself so they trust you enough to give you that guy's job?" Mason shot Ryan a glance. "You said he was good, but that's some seriously fast work."

"Actually," Brax said, "it's been a long time coming."

The room was silent for a beat. Then Mason said, "Holy shit. Are you saying what I think you're saying?"

"Mason, why don't you give me a few moments with Brax and Cami?"

"Will do."

"And Mason —"

"Not even Denny," Mason said. "You have my word." He shot Brax a look that seemed more supportive than shocked, then slipped out of Ryan's office.

"I'm so sorry," Cami said.

Ryan leaned back in his chair. "For accidentally revealing something to me?"

She grimaced. "There's really no way I end up looking good here, so I'm just going to stay quiet."

"Ryan and Mason both knew I ran cons before the FBI," Brax said. "No worries there."

"But Ryan didn't know that you were involved in the original heist," Ryan said. "It must have slipped your mind yesterday when you got sick."

Brax closed his eyes and counted to five. "The woman who was killed—she was my girlfriend. I should have told you that. And that I was on the original team. I didn't. I don't know why except that I was already off my game. September second is a pretty shitty day for me."

"I imagine it would be," Ryan said. "I'm sorry for your loss."

Brax blinked back tears. He'd expected a dressing down, not sympathy. He drew a breath, gathering himself. "You have no reason to believe me now, but the fact is, Cami and I came in today to get you up to speed. *Fully* up to speed. Backstory and all."

"All right," Ryan said. "Let's hear it."

So Brax told him. Everything. Meeting Sabrina in the Manhattan shelter. Growing up on the grift. Meeting Darrin and getting invited to be part of the team for the LA job. Moving out here. The heist going every which way of bad it possibly could.

Losing Sabrina.

Then losing himself.

It had been in those rough months when he'd been picked up for petty theft by the LAPD. But instead of being tried, he'd found himself talking with a man from a government office.

"I can't say what department. Just that it's covert and I agreed to come work for them. Cami did, too, though it was another month at least before she and I met. That department filtered agents to the FBI. It was a program that was looking to combine street smarts with regular training. Assuming you fit the profile. We did."

Ryan nodded slowly. "I appreciate you telling me. So you won't sit there shaking in your chairs, I'll let you know right off the bat that this changes nothing. If anything, it makes both of you more qualified for this job. But let me be clear. Leave out any kind of mission sensitive information again, and you'll be riding a desk for a year."

"Yes, sir."

He turned to Cami. "Was he telling the truth or covering for you? Were you in on the original heist, too?"

"No, sir. My past is far less interesting than Brax's."

Brax knew enough to know that wasn't entirely true. But he wasn't going to push her to reveal all. That was her decision. Besides, if the thoughtful look on Ryan's face was any indication, Ryan didn't believe her either. He didn't, however, push her. Not yet, anyway.

Instead, he turned back to Brax. "Tell me about your girlfriend and her twin."

Brax nodded, then slowly told him the entire story, impressed that he got through it without his throat clogging or needing to race once again to the men's room. "I walked away. The job had collapsed, and I went into self-preservation mode. So I disappeared. Now Samantha thinks I killed her sister. And so does Darrin. I can only presume Jorge will, too."

"She died on September second."

"Yes."

"I'm sorry to have put you through that yesterday."

"Well, I'm sorry not to have been forthright."

"Can you handle this assignment Agent Reed? Can you work with this woman and still keep your shit together?"

"Honestly? At first I wasn't sure. I am now." Not only was he confident he *could* do it, the truth was that he wanted to. If for no other reason than that by interacting with that team he might—just might—finally find some answers to what happened fifteen years ago.

"Anyway, that's where we are. First team meeting is tonight at the Pier. And this will be our last visit to the office. Too risky."

"Agreed." Ryan turned to face Cami. "Anything not already in your SSA file that you feel the need to share?"

"No, sir," she said, looking him straight in the eyes.

Ryan nodded, as if he believed her. Then again, why wouldn't he? Cami was an accomplished liar, after all.

Brax, however, had spent many a long night playing poker with her and Ollie. He knew her well. And he couldn't help but wonder what secret she was still holding so close.

A good thirty seconds passed in silence, and Brax started to wonder if he'd been wrong. Maybe Ryan really could see through Cami. Maybe he knew more about her than Brax did.

Finally, Ryan sat back, his hands folded on the table top. "Now it's my turn for a confession." He looked to each of them in turn. "Sensitive Operations Command. Mean anything to you?"

As Ryan spoke, Brax's blood turned cold. The SOC was the department that had taken him and Cami in, then filtered them to the FBI. He saw Cami turn toward him, and saw the effort it was taking to keep her expression blank.

"Don't bother answering," Ryan said. "I'm not trying to force you to break an oath. And I already know the answer, anyway." He stood up, then signaled them to do the same. "Follow me."

As he turned from them, Brax and Cami exchanged the kind of look that very clearly conveyed, *What the fuck?*

Unfortunately, neither of them had an answer.

Cami spoke up first. "Can I ask where we're going, sir?"

"Of course," Ryan said. "We're going to the helipad. And then we have a meeting with Colonel Seagrave."

CHAPTER TEN

I'd told Brax and Carly that I had errands to run, but that's not exactly true.

Or, rather, it's not even remotely true.

Still, the fact that I'm now at the Beverly Center swinging a shopping bag as I head for the elevator makes me blend in with the crowd. Just another girl doing some shopping before the lunchtime crowd shows up.

I slide into the elevator, grateful when no one jumps on before the doors close. I hit the button for the basement, then stand in the center of the car, tilt my head back so that I'm looking at the lighting panels on the ceiling, and count to ten.

I hear the familiar beep that signals that my retina scan was complete, and at the same time, the security panel beneath the buttons slides open, revealing an entirely different set of levels.

I hit the button for sub-basement four and the panel slides closed again, a sharp click making clear that it's locked back in place.

Maybe it's silly, but I love this part of my job. It reminds me of shows like *Kim Possible,* where there are all sorts of gadgets and the good guys always win.

I watch the floor indicator lights clicking past sub-1, sub-2, sub-3, then finally stopping at sub-4. The doors slide open and I glide out, swinging my shopping bag and actually grinning. I'm not usually this chipper coming to work, but I can't deny that I'm feeling good this morning. I know I owe that feeling to Brax, and I also know I probably shouldn't feel quite so giddy. After all, it's only my heart trying to convince me he had nothing to do with killing me.

My head knows better.

My head's seen the evidence.

If it's real.

I push the thought aside. Of course it's real. Why wouldn't it be?

If it means what they say it means. If it

wasn't just a long con to get you to join the group.

I frown, because how arrogant does *that* sound, and I order my brain to shut up while I walk the long hallway to the next checkpoint.

The "group" is my employer, Group Ultra, an elite branch of an already elite government organization called the Sensitive Operations Command, which runs covert operations under the supervision of Pentagon. Usually I'm stationed at the Eastern Division in Manhattan. But I was hand-selected for this op here at the Western Division in Los Angeles.

I pause for another retinal scan, then enter a janitor's closet after I hear the lock click open. I pull the lever beneath the sink, which opens a hidden door. I head into the newly revealed hall, walk for what feels like a year, and pass through the last set of security checks before pushing through what looks like a grimy, rusty door only to enter an absolutely stunning reception area decorated in Mid-Century Modern, with original artwork that would make a curator at the MOCA green with envy.

I've been in town a month doing prep work, and I know my way around the office now. I give Anna, the receptionist a quick wave. She holds up a finger, silently requesting that I wait as she reviews the video of my arrival.

When she's satisfied that I didn't have a tail, she gives me a thumbs-up, then remotely opens the steel doors the lead to the bullpen.

The irony of this job is that I wouldn't have it at all if Brax—or someone who framed Brax—hadn't decided to kill me.

I frown, realizing that from the moment I approached him at his apartment door, I've been giving Brax a mental out almost every time I think about that day.

I need to be careful. I need to be smart. I can't let the fact that I'm still attracted to him—still *very* attracted to him—affect my work. I want answers, yes. But I want real ones.

I need to think with my head. Not other parts of my body that have suddenly reawakened with a vengeance now that I'm around that man again.

I pause at my desk to drop off my purse, then look at the station next to me. The desktop is tidy, and the brass plate that says J. Ramos is polished to a sheen.

I grab a sticky note and draw a smiley face on it, then leave it on his desk. Ramos has been my mentor for the last fifteen years. I'm pretty sure this is the first time I've beat him to the office. Then again, maybe he's already here.

I frown, then look around, only to see Larry hurrying toward me. "Is Ramos around?" I ask.

Larry shakes his head, his currently orange hair pulled up into a topknot. "Haven't seen him. But the Big Dog is looking for you."

"You know he hates being called that."

"The hell he does. He loves it. *Woof. Woof.*"

"I've said it before, Larry. You may be the best tech guy on the planet, but you're seriously weird."

"That's my charm."

"Can't argue with that." He falls in step beside me as I head for the Egg, the oval-shaped conference room where briefings are held. "Did you see my memo?" I ask. "We're all in play now. Ramos and I are going to need an exit strategy. Me, especially. Cami and Brax are bound to be sticking close to me."

He grins. "You think I'm not already on that? Lambert's been breathing down my neck since you reported in. You think he's going to risk losing his best agent?"

I feel my cheeks warm. "I'm not his best agent," I say, then realize that Director Lambert has fallen in step beside us, his long, lean form eating up the ground as we move forward.

My cheeks get even warmer, and I hope he didn't overhear.

"Good to have you in from the field, Sabrina." His brown eyes are kind but stern "Ready for the briefing?"

"Absolutely," I say.

Lambert nods, then picks up his pace to walk a few steps in front of us. Larry just grins, then whispers, "Teacher's pet."

"And the meeting's on for tonight at the Pier," I say, ignoring him.

"On it," Larry says. "We can go over the specifics of what you might need in the way of tech after the briefing."

I give him a thumbs-up and hurry toward the Egg. Lambert's a fair man and an excellent boss, but he hates to be kept waiting.

He's also one of the people I respect most in the world, in large part because he saved my life. Not that I knew it was him until weeks after, but he had an operation that overlapped with the original heist. He learned about the van being wired, and he sent Ramos to warn me.

I hadn't believed him at first, but then Ramos pulled me aside and played a series of intercepted calls. Brax talking with another man. Planning an exit strategy in which they'd end up the only winners. And I was to be one of the sacrificial lambs.

I didn't believe it. Even fifteen years ago, a tape could be faked. But I still couldn't get it out of my mind. I watched Brax like a hawk, but there was nothing dodgy. At least not until that last day. When he didn't come back to the van. And even though I didn't want to believe that of him, self-preservation won out. I was just about to open the door when someone did it for me. It was Ramos, and he yanked me by the arm and pulled me clear just as the bomb ignited, sending flames screaming into the sky and singeing my clothes.

That's when I knew. I couldn't believe it, but I knew.

Brax had sold me out. The man I loved set me up to die, all so that he could get a bigger slice of the take from the heist.

By all rights, I should be dead now. Maybe it wasn't Brax who wired the van—I want so badly to believe that—but someone did. No doubt about that.

And if Lambert hadn't tasked Ramos to get me the hell out of there, I'd be nothing but dust,

my death marked only by a gravestone somewhere, if even that.

But I'm not dead. I'm alive, and I have a
stellar job that I love, great co-workers, and
Ramos has become one of my closest friends.

I don't have Brax, though.

Still, all things considered, I'm pretty damn
lucky.

———

"Now that I have you captive in the air," Ryan
said, his voice tinged with humor, "I can tell you
that I already knew about the heist, about the
SOC recruiting, and about the program with the
FBI. I learned of it three weeks ago."

Despite the din from the helicopter, Brax
had no trouble hearing Ryan's words through
the headphones they all wore. He glanced at
Cami, who looked just as surprised as Brax.

"Why didn't you say so ages ago," Cami
asked. "And why didn't anyone tell us. Nothing
personal, Mr. Hunter, but part of the agreement
when we joined was that all of this would
remain confidential."

"And I assure you it will. Colonel Seagrave
is the one who told me, and it was most defi-

nitely a need-to-know situation. Even so, you're right to feel annoyed, even betrayed. But let me assure you that I don't care what you did before. There's not a one of us who doesn't have things in our past we'd like to keep buried. No one else in the office other than Damien is aware. Share if you want — that's your prerogative—but as far as Stark Security is concerned, your past is irrelevant. All we care about is your work.

"What happened three weeks ago?" Brax asked after Cami just shrugged in response to his questioning glance.

"We'll be landing soon. We'll tell you all of it then."

Brax frowned, but nodded. He sat back in his seat and told himself not to panic. It was ridiculous, but he could feel that same terror rising the way it had when he was a kid and his dad would slide into one of his rages. The unpredictable kind that might earn Brax a mere spanking, a series of shoves holding his head under water, or the pain and smell of burning flesh that came when his father pressed the branding iron to the back of his thigh.

It was the same kind of fear he'd feel in later years when he'd be walking the street—not even thinking about a con, much less pulling one. But he'd see a cop and start to panic, certain the officer would scoop him up for no reason at all, then toss him into a dark cell just for the pleasure of punishing him.

He felt the light squeeze of his hand and realized he'd closed his eyes. He opened them to find Cami studying him. Her brow rose in question, and he nodded, silently telling her that he was okay. He hoped to hell he'd just told her the truth.

After fifteen minutes in the air, the copter descended to a roof long enough for them to get out before it rose back up into the sky. Brax looked around, but nothing was familiar. He knew only that they had to be somewhere in the LA area. And that didn't tell him much at all.

A door led to an elevator bank, and they got into the waiting car. There were no buttons and no floor indicator, but Brax could guess from the swift movement of the car and the lag it took from start to finish, that they were in one of the city's skyscrapers.

The doors opened onto a crisp, modern area with a polished stone floor and contemporary furniture in mostly leather and steel.

A pair of sliding doors parted, and Colonel Anderson Seagrave rolled through in his wheelchair. "Cami, Brax." His gruff voice was reassuring. "I'm sorry if we put you ill at ease, but it's wonderful to see you both again."

"It's great to see you, too, Colonel," Brax said. "And please don't take this the wrong way, but why the hell are we here?"

"You're currently undertaking to protect the Sisters against another attempted theft."

Brax glanced at Ryan. "That's correct."

"As it turns out, the mission is about more than merely protecting the Sisters. It's imperative those stones don't fall into the wrong hands."

Brax met Cami's eyes and saw that she was just as confused as he was.

"What I'm about to tell you is highly classified," Seagrave said. "The consequences, should this information leak, would be dire. Do you understand?"

"Of course. Whose wrong hands are we protecting them from?"

"Well, that's where it gets interesting," Seagrave says, shooting a half-smile toward Ryan.

As if taking his cue, Ryan swipes his arm in a circle. "From the SOC," he says.

Brax pinched the bridge of his nose. "The SOC. *This* SOC?"

"Actually, no," Seagrave said, then frowned, his expression turning completely grave. "It appears that we have a shadow."

"A shadow?" Cami repeated. "What does that mean?"

"A criminal organization—highly funded, extremely professional, and very organized. And it's passing itself off as an off-book division of this organization. Needless to say, the Pentagon is not pleased. We've been trying to locate their cell for months. We know enough to be certain there are cells in both Manhattan and Los Angeles. We believe Miami and San Francisco, too. London and Paris are also confirmed."

"Good god," Cami said, her voice barely a whisper.

"What's our assignment?" Brax asked. The SOC was the organization that had pulled him out of the morass of grief and crime he'd slid into after Sabrina had died. For that alone, he'd do whatever was necessary to stop the counterfeit group.

"We have reason to believe they're trying to steal the Sisters. We've had a deep cover agent in place now for almost two months, and his intel seems solid."

"You have an agent in place?" Cami repeated. "Then why haven't you burned them to the ground?"

"We need more evidence from every cell, not just one. And we need to know how many cells there are. Even with our mole, we're mostly flying blind. We're hoping to remedy that soon. In fact, we're hoping to capture one of their agents during your operation. The priority is to prevent the theft, of course, but lassoing an agent of the Los Angeles cell for interrogation would be an incredible coup."

"You think they're going to piggyback off the heist that we're planning?"

"Not piggyback. We think they're going to be in the thick of it, either monitoring your operation or actually have their players on the team."

"That's likely," Cami said. "Darrin and Jorge both served time. They might have been approached."

"Exactly," Seagrave said.

"For that matter," Ryan added, "it's possible they killed Tim because he wouldn't cooperate."

"And maybe they're the ones who killed Sabrina," Brax said, his voice almost a whisper.

"Quite possible," Ryan agreed. "And they probably intended to kill you, too."

"But that was fifteen years ago," Brax says. "If they wanted the sisters back then, why wait so long? Why didn't they raid Wolfe's home? Or the previous owner's?"

"Wolfe's security is exceptional," Seagrave said. "But the point is valid. Their fingers may not have been in the soup back then. We're merely speculating. My point is simply to be aware. They refer to themselves as Group Ultra-.They're incredibly well-funded—primarily through trafficking of weapons, drugs, and humans—and their agents are loyal."

"And aware?" Brax asked. "They know what kind of organization they work for?"

"The top tier, yes. As for the lower level agents, we think not. But we can't be sure."

"That's crazy," Cami said. "How could they not know?"

"It's not crazy," Brax says, seeing full well how it would play out. "I've done it. On a much smaller scale, sure. But it's just a long-term con. Elaborate, but that's the gooey milk chocolate center. You build a world with every con. A decent conman keeps it small. The world exists in the story they tell. A mediocre conman might set up shop. Hang out a sign. Provide some bull-shit service. Pay a few panhandlers to pose as employees or customers. Setting the stage, but it's still just putting on a show. Anyone too clever just looks behind the curtain. A master conman, though..."

He looks around at the group. "At that level, it's not a stage anymore. It's not even a Disney ride. It's like walking into an AI generated world. Completely immersive." He exhaled, then met Seagrave's eyes. "If they have money and resources, then hell, yeah, they could pull it off. And their marks won't even see them coming."

CHAPTER ELEVEN

I take my seat in the briefing room around the huge conference table. Larry takes the seat beside me, and next to him is Director Lambert's personal assistant, his pen poised to take notes.

Lambert's standing beside the screen, his brow furrowed as he reviews a briefing bound in the familiar purple cover that designates it as a high priority mission.

On the other side of me is an empty chair, and beyond that is the newest guy on the team, Morris Grey, a recent transfer from Eastern Division. Since I've been in the field, I've only met him once, but he seems like a sharp guy. I hope so. We're a small team, but the work we do here is important, and everyone pulls their share of the weight.

I hear the door open behind me, and I turn as Ramos hurries in. I look down, hiding my smile. In all the years I've known him, the only time Ramos was ever early was when he pulled me out of the van with only seconds to spare.

"I'm buying you a watch for Christmas," I whisper to him as he slides into the seat beside me. "And I'm setting it fifteen minutes fast."

At the front of the room, Lambert's brows rise. "Thank you so much for joining us, Agent Ramos."

"Happy to be here." He leans back, smiling his familiar grin.

Lambert scowls, but I know he's not really angry. Ramos is a stellar agent, and around here, what counts most is the quality of your work. That and being a team player.

He presses a button on the lectern, and the lights dim as a screen descends from the ceiling. A moment later, an image appears. The Sisters.

"Since Mr. Grey is new to the team," Lambert says, "I'll do a brief recap. As most of you know, about fifteen years ago, these diamonds were the subject of an attempted heist."

Grey leans toward me. "I read your file," he says. "That was a wild ride that led you here."

"I can't argue with that," I say, then make a show of sitting back and zipping my lip when Lambert glares at us, one brow cocked.

"The leader of that team is making another go at stealing the stones. Darrin Gold isn't a particularly skilled thief, but he is a determined one. Agent Fox's mission is to see that that heist happens," he says firmly, nodding to me. "Those stones need to go missing."

"Why?" Grey asks.

"We've learned of a plot by a group of Eastern European terrorists to steal the Sisters when they're in transit from the Performing Arts Center where they will be on display back to the home of Kingston Wolfe."

"Going to be hard to find a buyer for those rocks," Grey says.

"They don't intend to sell the diamonds. They're acquiring the Sisters for use in a proto-type long-range laser weapon. They intend to use the weapon in an assault on the US and British embassies in Paris.

Grey's eyes wide. "Lasers." He looks around the room. "Is this some sci-fi fantasy?"

Lambert doesn't smile. "How often fiction

becomes fact."

"Diamonds have some pretty amazing properties," Larry says. "Remember that space laser in *Diamonds Are Forever?*" He looks around the room to find only blank faces. "James Bond. Come on. No one else has seen that?"

He waits another beat, then shakes his head in disappointment. "Point being, diamonds have insane thermal conductivity. That and their strength and optical properties—well, I just mean that the tech exists for cool weapons like that. What I wouldn't give to study their prototype..."

"Thank you, Larry," Lambert says dryly. "With luck, we'll be able to acquire the weapon and the specs. But our first order of business is to prevent it becoming operational. Apparently it needs a diamond of a certain quality, and the Sisters are a perfect match."

Grey nods. "So the team Agent Fox pulled together is infiltrating Gold and his team in order to keep them from stealing the Sisters for these terrorists?"

"Precisely. As Agent Fox suspected, Darrin Gold was already considering taking another run at it. She gave him a little nudge and now the operation is set. The diamonds will only be on display opening night. After that, Wolfe intends to replace them with counterfeits, though the general public won't know that. We'll let the heist succeed, then Sabrina will ensure that the Sisters make their way to us, while the stones Darrin's team retains are excellent fakes."

"And when Gold discovers their quality, he'll assume the ones on display were a decoy," I add. "That Wolfe chickened out and never put the real Sisters on display."

"Our hope is this pro-active heist will keep Wolfe safe and also flush out the terrorists so that we can finally corral all the members of that network," Lambert adds.

"Complex, but it should work," Grey says. "But once the terrorists realize they don't have the real diamonds, won't they raid Wolfe's house?"

"A possibility," Lambert says. "Of course, the government will provide protection. I believe the Director is already in communication with the CIA and FBI about that very possibility."

Grey nods, clearly relieved.

"The plan will work," Ramos says from my other side. "With this team, we can't miss."

"Speaking of teams," I say. "I'm meeting with the heist group today at seven."

"Excellent," Lambert says. "And the members are?"

"Same as before for the most part. That worked out well. Jorge, obviously," I say, pointing to Ramos. "Darrin, me, Brent Travers," I add, calling him by the name they know him from the file. "And there's a new girl he's recruited. Carly Jamison. I ran her. She's got mad skills and a dicey background. I don't expect trouble from her, and frankly making an issue out of Brent's choice would have raised some red flags."

I ignore the way Lambert is looking at me. But when I meet Ramos' eye, I can see that he's surprised, too. Well, too bad. This is my op, and I'll run it my way. She's going to be assigned outside the center and away from the switch. It will be fine.

I say none of that aloud, but I do give Ramos my *I know what I'm doing* glare. He spreads his hands as if silently acknowledging that this is my op to run my way.

I'm afraid Lambert will be less kind, but he says nothing, either. In fact, all he does say is that Stark Security has been hired to protect the Sisters. "Don't underestimate them."

"I won't," I assure him. I'm familiar with Stark Security's reputation. I've even thought that it would be an interesting place to work. Not that I'm looking to change jobs. I love working at Group Ultra. The work is exciting and fascinating. More than that, it's important.

We're a deep cover branch of the Sensitive Operations Command, a covert organization with oversight by the Pentagon. Only a very few SOC agents even know we exist. It's hard, dangerous work, and I love it.

I love the purpose it gives me. Not just to make money—though the pay is nothing to sneeze at—but to know I'm using all the skills I learned on the street for good. Not to steal food or money or con my way into a place to sleep for a night, but to make the world a better place.

I love my teammates, too. Lambert's strict but fair. And I owe him and Ramos everything.

I still don't know why Group Ultra was watching our heist, or how they'd even gotten wind of it. But I'm glad they did. And even though I'd protested when they told me that there was a bomb—and that Brax had planted it —they still stood by me, with Ramos right there in that split-second when I'd decided not to be a fool and get the hell out of the van.

Even now, I can feel the heat of that explosion as vividly as the horror I felt knowing Brax had planted it. In those first days, I assumed that Brax realized I'd escaped. After all, surely he could see through the windshield. I feared he'd seek me out. Tell me he that loved me and had been terrified I'd died. Cry and say how relieved he was that I'd survived.

And when he did all that, I'd just spit in his face.

But I learned from another operative that the sun's glare blocked any vision of me. Brent—well, Brax—believed I died in the explosion. Just as Group Ultra had told me he'd planned.

I'd been a wreck at first. The man I'd loved had killed me, after all. But Jorge Ramos had been my anchor. He'd been at Group Ultra for two years at that point, and I owe the ease of my transition to him.

He'd paid a hard price, though. He served prison time for the heist—something that had been part of the plan so he could continue to gain the trust of the original team members. But even when he was behind bars, we kept in touch, and I knew he would help me whenever I needed.

Now, he asks if pulling Brax into the heist really made sense. "Seems dangerous. He knows you too well."

"I want him there," I say. "He tried to kill me. I want him to see that he failed. That I'm doing just fan-fucking-tastic without him. And whatever he thought he'd gain, doesn't look like it happened. So all he did was flip a woman who loved him to a woman who hates him." I say the words like I mean them, because when this all started, I did.

I tell myself that I'm not having doubts. But of course I am.

Right now, though, I don't have the luxury of letting anyone know that.

Ramos studies my face. "All right, I get that. But no matter what personal baggage you two have, we all have to work together. This time, we really need to steal that stone. It can't go back to Wolfe's house. Not with those commandoes waiting to swoop in and take the sisters from him."

I look between him and Lambert. "I can handle it," I say. And I really hope that's not a lie.

CHAPTER TWELVE

E ven though Jorge and I leave the Group
Ultra office at the same time, I show up
at the Santa Monica Pier fifteen minutes before
he's scheduled to arrive. We decided that he'd
get "stuck in traffic" simply so that we wouldn't
arrive together. After all, we're not supposed to
have even seen each other since the botched
heist fifteen years ago.

It's doubtful that anyone would notice if we
did, or even if they did notice that they'd think
anything of it. But in this business, you learn to
be overly careful.

That's what keeps you alive.

The plan was to meet at seven, but I arrive
five minutes early. The Pier is huge and

crowded, with way more rides than I remember from fifteen years ago.

Not that I'm surprised. Things change, after all. Fortunately for me, though, the old-timey carousel hasn't changed much. It's still there, and still as charming as ever. It's also our designated meeting spot. I head that way, glancing around to see if Brax is here yet.

I don't see him, though, so I pull out my phone and wander around taking a few pictures, just so I look like a tourist. I'm about to circle to the back of the carousel when I hear Brax's laugh behind me. I turn and see him and Cami standing together near a refreshment booth watching a young kid doing crazy gymnastics to the delight of everyone standing around.

As I watch, Cami claps for the kid, then tosses a bill into the cap he's put on the ground near his fast-moving feet. She backs away, bumping into Brax, he steadies her by hooking his arm around her waist.

I freeze, completely undone by the unexpected flood of pure, sharp jealousy that crashes over me. I suck in a breath, force myself to stay focused, and shove that jealousy straight out of my head.

I'd like to say that the skills I've learned in

my time with Group Ultra make that easy, but that would be a lie. The skills make it possible. But it's not easy. Because as much as I wish it weren't true, this jealousy is real.

Leave it to me to still be in love with a man who may well have tried to kill me.

Except I'm *not* in love with him, I tell myself, though I can't say that I'm terribly convincing.

More than that, I'm no longer convinced he did try to kill me. On the contrary, I'm a confused mess, which is not only an emotional pain in the ass but is also making it genuinely hard to remain objective during this mission.

I know I should tell Lambert about all this emotional goo that's tumbling around inside of me. At the very least, I should tell Jorge.

But I know I'm not going to. They'd both say I need to be taken off this mission. More, that I need to go back to New York. They'd pull out all the evidence they have that he either planted the bomb or knew about it. The fact that Jorge saw him fiddling with a tire on the van, only later realizing that he must have been using the tire as a decoy to get up under the car. The "delay" text from me, so easily fabricated. And something I never saw—the record of Tim's interrogation before he was shivved, wherein he said that he'd learned that Brax and Darrin had conspired to get rid of the other team members so they could keep the payout for themselves. But that record could be entirely made up. It's not on video, after all. And Tim's not alive to authenticate it.

"Sam!"

I turn toward Cami, who's hurrying toward me.

"You looked lost in thought. Everything okay?"

"Oh, sure," I lie. "I was just thinking about how much has changed since the last time I was here." That, at least, is more or less true. And that, of course, is the secret for telling a good lie. Seed it with something true.

I look around. "Where's Brax?"

"Got a text." She checks her watch. "Are we that early? Where are Darrin and Jorge?"

"I don't know about Darrin, but Jorge texted that he's stuck in traffic. Darrin probably is, too."

As we talk, Cami leads us to the refreshment stand and orders a Coke. I get a Popsicle just for the nostalgia of it.

Once we have our snacks, we move aside. Cami has an empty water bottle hanging from her shoulder in one of those gizmos that goes around the neck so that the cap holds the strap in place. She tucks the soda under her arm, takes the lid off, then hands the metal water bottle to me.

"I hate drinking out of plastic," she says, then opens the Coke and pours it into the bottle that I hold still for her. "Honestly, the more you get to know me, the more of my charming and lovable quirks you'll get acquainted with."

Despite my lingering jealousy—yes, I can admit it—I smile. "Looking forward to it," I say, surprised that I mean it.

She takes a sip of her soda, and for a moment, silence lingers. I'm not sure if I'm desperate for an answer or just looking to fill the quiet, but I hear myself blurt out, "So, did you guys date?"

If Cami thinks the question is rude, she doesn't show it. She just shakes her head, as if the question is totally whacky. Relief starts to flood my body, only to shift to an icy chill when she says. "We slept together for a while, but it was just a friends-with-benefits thing. Never serious."

"Oh," I say.

She cocks her head. "It was over years and years ago."

"Oh, please," I say, trying to sound casual. "It doesn't matter to me. And it's none of my business anyway."

Cami nods. "Well, then I really shouldn't have said anything." I see the hint of a grin tugging at her mouth. "I'm sure Brax will be annoyed as hell with me, but I only mentioned it because I thought it *was* your business."

I frown, completely confused. "What do you mean?"

She shrugs, then takes a long sip of soda before responding. "Just that I figured it was only fair that you know. I mean, since you're attracted to him."

"What?" I almost choke on the sip of water I'd just taken. "I'm not attracted to him."

Cami actually laughs. "Oh, please. Cons were never my thing. You have to be able to read such subtle nuances in people. But even I can read you well enough to know that you're lying. And why wouldn't you be? He's awesome."

"But not for you." I make it a statement, not a question.

She lifts her hands in a *what can you do* gesture. "Oh, I love him. I just don't *love* him.

He's my best friend, but I'm not in love with him. And I never have been."

I want to ignore the powerful wave of relief that threatens to knock me over. I shouldn't care who Brax loves or who he sleeps with. I'm only here for the mission, then I'm going back to New York and the thing I really do love—my job at Group Ultra.

I *want* to ignore it, but I can't. Because it's real. I'm happy—hell, I'm giddy—to learn that there's nothing but friendship between Brax and Cami.

I only realize how deep I've slipped into the emotional danger zone when I hear myself asking, "Is he seeing someone else, then?"

She shakes her head, but she doesn't laugh this time. Instead, her expression is as serious as I've seen since I met her. "I wish he was. He needs to get over her, but I'm starting to wonder if he ever will."

My mouth has gone completely dry. "Sabrina."

She nods, then looks at my face and winces. "I'm so sorry. I shouldn't have brought her up. I know it hurts you, too."

"No," I say, forcing a smile. "It's okay. And—and I do feel bad for him, not being able to move on. But in some horrible, selfish way, it makes me happy to know that Sabrina had someone who loved her so, so much."

I taste salt and realize that I'm crying. I frown, then wipe the tears away. "Sorry," I say, but Cami just shakes her head, her smile tender.

I wish Brax and the others would join us so that we can get on with it. I want to talk work so that I can stop the spiral of thoughts and emotions twirling in my head. Because right now, I don't know what to think.

"What about you?" I blurt, wanting desperately to change the subject. "You're not with Brax, but are you with someone?"

"No," Cami says. The word is firm and seems to hold an encyclopedia's worth of meaning. I want to ask, but I already know that I won't get an answer.

Thankfully, the awkward silence is broken when Brax returns. "I finally got a text back from Darrin. He was in a dead zone in the canyons. Got stuck behind a wreck. Said he'll be another fifteen minutes at least. I have a feeling Jorge may be in that same traffic jam."

"In that case, I'm going to find a restroom," Cami says. I'm about to say that I'll join her, but Brax grins at me and suggests we hop on a ride.

"Seriously?"

"Why not? Everyone else on the Pier is having fun. And Brina loved amusement parks." His eyes narrow as he studies me. "Did you two have that in common?"

"Hardly. They've always scared me. Not the ride itself," I amend. "The fact that I have no idea who's maintaining them."

That's kind of a lie. I've always been leery. But in the Sabrina-times, I never wanted to show fear, so I'd ride anyway. I still feel the same way, but I need to keep up the illusion that we're different people. And, perversely, I want to see how Brax reacts to a woman who's not as apparently gung-ho and fearless as the girl he loved.

"How about we let you pick the ride, and I'll promise to keep you safe?"

I grin, amused. "You're the Amusement Park Police?"

"Yes, ma'am," he says, whipping off a military salute.

I fight a laugh. "Okay, but if my screams burst your eardrums, you only have yourself to blame."

He glances around the Pier. "Pacific Plunge or the roller coaster?"

I glance at the two rides. The roller coaster is fast and twisty. The Plunge takes you up in a big bucket, then basically drops you. It's like the Tower of Terror at Disney World, a ride which I think is very aptly named.

I mentally suck in a deep breath for courage. "Definitely the Plunge," I say. "It's way more of a thrill."

He meets my eyes, then holds them. "Yeah," he says, his voice so soft I'm not sure he's talking about the ride. "There's something about falling and not knowing if anyone will be there to catch you." He closes his eyes, and I see his throat move as he swallows.

When he opens his eyes again, his gaze seems to burn into mine. "I miss your sister."

"Me, too," I whisper, more moved by his words than I want to be. Because the truth is, I want to believe him. Not just the words, but the emotions. I want to believe that he really felt what he says he did.

"Wait here," he says. "I'll run get the tickets."

I watch as he goes to the ticket counter, trying to wrap my head around all the facts and emotions and possible lies that have been surrounding me since I showed up in front of his apartment.

I know he's that good of an actor — there's no way we could have pulled off the kind of cons we did if he wasn't. But I also know his technique. I know his heart.

And those words had the ring of truth in them.

But even if I'm right, what does that mean? Just because he misses me doesn't exonerate him. He still could have killed me.

Except the possibility feels false and leaves a bitter taste.

If Cami's right, Brax really did love me beyond all reason, just like I'd believed—just like I'd loved him. And if that's the case, there's no way on earth he would have killed me, not even if it saved himself.

And how ironic is that? The whole reason I'd been excited about this assignment was that it positioned me for revenge. Revenge I craved because I'd lost faith in the man I loved. Now, I may well have burned a bridge I'll never be able to repair.

It's not revenge I want anymore. Or at least, not against Brax. Instead, I want answers.

Maybe I'm a fool.

Maybe I'm thinking with parts of my body other than my brain.

But I believe him. I don't think he had anything to do with the bomb.

But if that's the case, then who really killed me? And now that I'm back—albeit as my sister —I can't help but wonder if my foiled killer is going to try again?

CHAPTER THIRTEEN

W e've been waiting in the line for ten minutes, talking and laughing, when we're finally ushered into the little compartment with a few other thrill seekers. It's open, with only a strap and a bar to hold us in.

"You swear you won't let me fly out," I say, trying to make the restraint as tight as possible.

He grins. "If you do, I'll fly out with you."

"Like that would do any good."

"Hey, you jump, I jump."

I laugh. "You don't even like *Titanic*."

He frowns. "Sabrina told you *that*?"

I laugh, but inside I'm cursing my slip-up. "I told you we talked about everything."

"Yeah, well, maybe it's grown on me. In

some ways I feel like Jack. I let go and sank away, and she's the one who's really still living."

I blink, fighting tears. Until that moment, we'd been laughing and goofing around. It had felt so easy when we were standing in line. It had felt like we were *us* again. Brent and Sabrina. And nothing in the world could touch us.

As if he can see the direction my thoughts have taken, he shakes his head as he says, "Sorry. Didn't mean to toss a downer into the ride."

"No, it's okay. You didn't. Oh, *shit!*" The car's started to rise—at more or less a snail's pace—and Brax isn't alone when he laughs at my reaction. The others in our little box giggle, too.

I roll my eyes. "I told you I'm a wimp."

He twines his fingers with mine. "And I told you that I've got you."

I turn to face him, my heart swelling. I want to tell him everything, but I can't. Even though I believe him—and yes, somehow everything inside me has flipped, and I really do believe him—I can't say a thing. This isn't just an ex-boyfriend sitting next to me. He's one of a group who are intending to steal the Sisters.

For all I know, he's even involved with the terrorists who want to ultimately acquire the diamonds. Except, of course, he's not. After all, I'm the one who pulled him into the heist. Which also makes him one of the heroes who's going to protect the Sisters. Just like me.

The only difference is he thinks he's committing a crime, whereas I know I'm working for the good guys.

"Where'd you go?" He's tilted his head in that way he does when he's trying to figure something out. "I think I lost you."

I laugh. "Believe me, I'm not going anywhere now. But I am checking out the view." I nod toward the Pacific spread out before us, aglow with the light of the sun as it slips below the horizon. I twist around and up, trying to see how much higher we're going, but I can't quite see. And isn't that a tidy metaphor for my life at the moment?

Because I have no idea where any of this is taking me.

I turn to smile at him, only to see him looking at me with an expression of longing so familiar I have to stifle a gasp. "Brax," I say before I can even think. And right then, I'm absolutely certain that he's going to kiss me.

He leans closer, his eyes locked on mine. Then closer still.

And that's when I scream.

Not because he's kissing me, but because we're falling, careening down, about to crash onto the Pier at a velocity that will turn us all to mush.

Brax clasps my hand, and I squeeze back, so hard I'm probably breaking all his fingers.

And then it's over. The fall. The connection. The possibility of a kiss. All swept away by the velocity of our descent.

Before I know it, we're off the ride and standing on the Pier as tourists and locals swarm around us, the crowd having increased with the setting sun.

Brax swipes his fingers through his hair. "I guess I owe you an apology."

I shake my head. "No. No, it's fine."

"It's just that—" He cuts himself off with a frown and pulls out the burner phone. "Cami," he says. "The others are here, but they're heading down to the beach. Too crowded up here."

"Let's go," I say, starting to head that direction and grateful to avoid whatever he'd intended to say.

"You're so much like her," he tells me.

"From what I've seen, you're fearless. But the little things..."

"That drop was not a little thing."

He laughs. "She was terrified of cockroaches."

"I know. And I don't blame her one bit." That is one fear I'm not about to pretend I don't share.

"And for some reason, the light through Venetian blinds freaked her out."

"Our father. The room he kept us in had a window too high for us to reach. It had Venetian blinds. When the sun was coming through in slats, we knew that he'd be coming for us soon."

He pauses, taking my arm and tugging me to a stop beside him. "She never told me that."

I shrug. I hadn't liked to share too much of my horrific childhood with him. I don't know why. Maybe because it was so ugly that I was afraid the ugliness would rub off on me. He knew all of the big picture stuff, though. The child's coloring book version of my life. But I'd kept the intricate adult coloring image all to myself.

I start walking again, and he doesn't stop me. But as we get closer to the sign that welcomes visitors to the Pier, he says, almost too soft for me to hear, "I'm glad you showed up."

It's me who stops this time, making the family of five behind us split up to go around. I ignore their dirty looks.

"That first moment," he continues, "when I realized you weren't actually Brina ... that was like sliding into hell. But now...." He draws a breath, and I watch as he gathers himself. "I've missed her so much, but part of that was guilt."

"Guilt?" I tense. I've convinced myself he was innocent. Is he about to confess now?

"For being alive. For not being in the van where I was supposed to be. And for not making her tell me more about what was bothering her that day." He meets my eyes again. "For not being a hero and saving her."

"You couldn't have. You didn't know."

He nods. "I know that. I do. Doesn't mean I don't hurt."

"Yeah. I get that."

"You're not her," he says. "But it's like you're a balm. But I'm not sure if the scabs are finally healing, or if the pain will be even more intense once you leave."

Leave.

The word hangs there, big and ugly. Of

course, I'll leave. That's what I'd wanted. To come here, find the truth, and make him pay.

As for the possibility that he's actually inno-cent, well, a day ago, I would have told myself that was impossible. Now...

Well, now I believe him.

But is that because he's truly innocent? Or do I just want to believe this man who, for better or for worse, I really do still love?

———

Brax watched as Jorge walked up to Samantha, shaking his head and looking amazed. "I don't think I really believed it until this moment," he said. "You're really alive."

"Looks that way," she said, taking his extended hand.

"I'm glad," he said. "I can't say I enjoyed getting picked up, convicted, and shoved into prison, but I kept thinking it was a hell of a lot better than being dead."

"I hear the food's better, too," Samantha said, making the entire group laugh.

"And as for you," Jorge continued, turning toward Brax. "You managed to escape death and prison. You get out of paying your taxes, too?"

Despite the light words, there was an edge to his voice.

"Still working on that," Brax said, keeping his response intentionally light. No way in hell was he apologizing for having survived as a free man. "I took the coward's way out and ran. Then I went under. But I might as well have been in prison. Brina was dead, and I damn sure felt like I was, too."

Jorge looked him up and down. "You didn't plant that bomb."

"I didn't."

He turned to Samantha. "And you believe him, too?"

"Does it matter? I'm here for the job. I lost out on a damn good payout when the last time we tried this went south. Not to mention the hoops I had to jump through to stay dead. And it's not as if I can just suddenly come back to life. I need my cut so I can disappear again. Trust me when I say that the dead have to pay for food and lodging, too."

She was good, Brax thought. A little too good, because she'd convinced him as well. And the truth was that he didn't want her going away again. Or, to be more accurate, he didn't want *Samantha* disappearing from his life. Not because he was projecting Sabrina onto her, but because the woman herself was getting under his skin.

"Let's get on with it," Darrin said. "Assignments, and then we're out until the next meeting."

"We'll do a dry run on Wednesday," Brax said. "That gives each of us the weekend and early next week to prepare and gather any tech or tools we need. I've got a source who can get us the schematics for the Gleason Center's security system, so Sabrina and I will go walk the Center tomorrow evening after we've had a chance to review them.

He looked at her for confirmation, and she nodded.

"I've got a source who can get us uniforms that match on-site security," Cami said. "And I may be able to get a list of which security guards have been selected to work the gala."

"That would be a coup," Jorge said. "Knowing how many and where they'll be stationed can help us map the plan."

Darrin stepped forward. "Let me toss a monkey into the wrench." He looked at each of them in turn. "We know the Sisters are coming to the gala from Kingston Wolfe's private vault.

And we know where he lives. All we need to learn is who's transporting them and the route. Then we swoop in and snatch them."

Jorge shook his head. "I don't know. Disabling security on a display case in a center that's not even set up like a museum is going to be much easier than breaking into an armored car."

"True, but Wolfe lives in the canyons. We'll have stretches of road with very little traffic, especially since the transfer will likely take place pre-dawn."

"It's not a bad idea," Jorge conceded.

Brax caught Samantha's eye. She shrugged. So did Cami.

"Alright, let's give it time to gel. Everyone, map out a plan if we go with an in-transit heist. We'll meet tomorrow and make our decision. Meanwhile, let's finish the briefing for the original plan."

Everyone agreed, and he quickly worked through the agenda, making sure everyone knew their roles and what needed to be in place before the gala. "I know two weeks can feel like forever, but it will be here before we know it. Cami, have at least three possible getaway routes mapped by tomorrow."

She nodded. "And we need at least two rehearsals, no matter which plan we go with." She looked at all of them in turn. "I heard about last time. Nothing can go wrong this go-round." She aimed a sharp look at Samantha, who picked up the thread.

"I'm probably an idiot for doing this," Samantha said. "Any one of you could have planted that bomb."

"Or you could have planted it yourself," Cami says.

"Excuse me?" Samantha snapped.

"What the hell?" Brax asked. "Why would she do that?"

Cami shrugged. "To get out of a bad situation."

A hot wire of fury cut through Brax. Not only was this *not* something they'd rehearsed, and the very idea that Sabrina would either kill herself or fake her own death was ridiculous. Especially since, by Cami's definition, he would be an integral part of the "bad situation."

Cami looked from him to all the rest of them. "Point being, it could have been any one of you. None of us know the why. Which means it could happen again." She shrugged casually, as if she hadn't managed to push the buttons of everyone standing in that circle. "I'm just saying we all need to be careful. And we need to trust each other."

They wrapped the meeting quickly after that, and Darrin and Jorge drifted away. Cami was about to follow, but Brax held her back.

"What the hell, Cami? What. The. Hell?

Cami tugged her arm free. "You're not at the top of your game, Brax." She shot a quick look to Samantha, silently telling him that she knew why he was supposedly off.

"Dammit, Cam—"

"She's *not* Sabrina. She's Samantha—no, just listen. She's Samantha, but they don't know that. They think she's the real, authenticated Sabrina. To them, Sabrina really did survive. And if that's the case, then she was either the luckiest person on the planet or she had warning and got out."

"Shit," he said, following her train of thought.

"And if I came to that conclusion, then so will they. We need to lay it out there. We need to tell them which it was. Otherwise it will fester and they won't trust Sam ... and by default you or me."

"I must have had a warning," Samantha said. "That kind of luck's not believable."

"Then who tipped you off?"

They all looked at each other.

"Tim," Brax finally said. "He's the only one that makes sense. And since he's dead he's not going to argue."

CHAPTER FOURTEEN

The ride back to Brax's apartment seems to take forever. I don't know what he's thinking about, but ever since he held my hand on the Pacific Plunge, my mind has been going down some very naughty paths.

Except that's not exactly accurate. The truth is, I've wanted him since I first got this assignment, although I haven't included that little tidbit in any of the reports I've submitted to Group Ultra.

And—who am I kidding?—even *that* isn't accurate. The truth is, I never got over him. I guess that makes me one of those pathetic women who still wants the man who hurt them. Except in my fantasies, it would almost always turn out it had never been him at all. He'd come to me, explaining that someone had double-crossed him. And even if I let my fantasies run with the idea that he really had been out to kill me, in my version of the story, he suffered so desperately from guilt and shame that seeing me alive has broken him. He wants only to make it up to me to and will do anything to prove his love.

Anything at all. *An-y-thing.*

It made for some tantalizing late-night fantasies.

But that's nothing compared to the real thing. And the truth is that now that I've convinced myself that he really was innocent in the bombing, all I want is to get him back.

I can't tell him the truth, though. For one, all I have is a gut feeling. And while I trust my gut, I don't think Group Ultra will be too pleased if I turn in a report saying that I've been sleeping with one of the men on the heist team I put together so that we could protect the very diamonds that he and I once tried to steal.

I could be wrong, but I'm thinking that's a no-no in my line of work.

Then again, who says I have to tell? After all, I'm—

"—or just stay here all night."

Brax's voice yanks me from my thoughts. Which, frankly, is probably a good thing. I take a breath to pull myself together, then turn to face him. "Sorry, what?"

Brax's face practically glows from the power of his grin. "I was just saying that we should either go inside or make up our minds to just stay here in the parking lot all night."

"Right. Sorry." I shift in my seat, certain my cheeks must be bright red. I think I even half-dozed off, lost in my thoughts. In the fantasies that keep peeking in around the edges.

Please, please don't let me have talked out loud.

"As comfortable as Old Blue is, I'm going to vote we go inside." I congratulate myself on my light tone, then slip out of the car without looking at him again, just in case he can read the truth in my eyes.

He probably can.

He always could before.

We're out of the car and walking across the parking area toward the street when he says, "It's still early, and we didn't eat. Want to walk around the corner to Blacklist?"

I almost say yes, but the truth is that I'm tired of being with him around other people. He may not be mine anymore, but I want a few minutes just to ourselves. "Would it be terrible if I said I'd rather stay in with pizza, a bottle of wine, and a movie?"

"Action ? Comedy? Psychological thriller?"

Considering the way my mind was going earlier, I almost suggest something ridiculously steamy. Like *Body Heat*. Instead I tell him that he can make the call.

He nods, says he'll think about it, and when we reach his door, he suggests *9 1/2 Weeks*. "I decided to go with psychological thriller," he says, with absolutely no irony in his voice.

Since that was our go-to movie as horny sixteen-year-olds, and we'd watch it whenever we managed to wrangle access to a television and CD player, I enthusiastically—but not *too* enthusiastically—agree.

"How about pizza? What's your flavor?"

"Pepperoni," I say automatically.

"With mushrooms?" He looks hopeful.

I laugh, then shake my head. "Sorry. Brina and I were identical in that respect, too. We both hate mushrooms."

He chuckles. "Well, damn. And here I thought you were an upgrade."

I swallow, but I say nothing. I force myself

not to react at all. But this is the first time I've
heard him say anything about my death that
wasn't heartbreaking. Not that I want him to
dance with joy at the thought of me being dead,
but I don't want him to continue being tortured,
either.

"I'm the deluxe model," I tell him. "And the
deluxe model is perfectly happy to pick the
mushrooms off."

His brows rise. "Really?"

I nod. I'd much rather not—mushrooms are
slimy and gross—but I figure that's why forks
were invented. And, honestly, in all the years
we were together, I never let him order mushrooms on a damn pizza. It's time to give the man
a break.

Soon enough, we have our pizza. I've
changed into my comfy shorts and a tank top,
and he's wearing sweats and a faded and
tattered Guggenheim tee that I actually
remember him buying. "This is nice," I say,
reaching for a slice as Mickey Rourke checks out
Kim Basinger.

"We used to watch this every chance we
got," he says when we're about halfway
through the movie. He's turned to look at me,
and I feel my breath hitch. At first, I think he

really means it when he says *we*. Then I understand he's talking about him and Sabrina. A
Sabrina who's definitely not in the room
with him.

"She told me," I say. "She, um, liked
watching it with you."

From the way he laughs, I know he hears all
the subtext. It was their—our?—foreplay.
Confused teens living on the street and
watching racy movies. Sometimes even
watching in some poor vacationer's house on
those rare occasions when we lucked out and
managed to break in.

When I reach for my wine, I realize he's still
looking at me and not the screen. I tilt my head,
intending to say something funny, but instead
my breath catches in my throat.

He looks away, but not before I see the heat
in his eyes.

Please, I think, wanting this far too much.
*Please don't let him think so much about Sabrina
that he feels guilty.*

A silence that feels heavy with possibility
settles between us as we eat pizza, drink wine,
and watch the rest of the movie. When it's over,
I shift my position on the sofa so that my back is
against the armrest and I'm facing him. My feet

are on the cool leather, my knees up, and my arms around my legs.

"We have a long day tomorrow," he says.

"Funny how so many tasks pile up when you're working as a criminal mastermind."

His lips twitch. "Isn't it just?"

"If you were asking if I'm tired," I say, "I'm not."

His eyes meet mine. They stay there. "It's not that late." He tilts his head, just a little. "Do you want to go out?"

I know him so well—or, at least, I *knew* him so well—but I still can't quite get a read on him. Are we flirting? Dancing around a naughty proposition? Or does he really want to go out for a drink or a slice of cheesecake for dessert?

I have no idea, so I do the only thing I can do. I tell the truth. "No. I want to stay in."

"All right," he says. "We'll stay here."

The silence hangs awkwardly between us, and I'm overwhelmed by the insane urge to just blurt out everything. That I'm Sabrina. That I believe that he didn't plant that bomb. That I'm sorry I didn't believe it from the beginning. That I miss him terribly. And that right then, the only thing I want more than for him to be kissing me is for him to be naked beside me in his bed.

Of course, I say none of that.

It's one of the ironies of life. I can be absolutely fucking fearless on the street. And yet when faced with a man I know used to love me, I revert to the awkwardness of a pre-teen.

Humans really are the most confusing of animals.

He watches as I take another sip of my wine.

"Don't," I say. "You're making me nervous."

"You have the prettiest mouth."

"Oh. Thank you."

He slides a little bit closer, then takes my wine from me, and puts it on the table. Then he brushes the pad of his thumb over my lower lip. And, honestly, that's when I'm a goner.

"Is this okay?" His tone suggests that he knows it is.

"Yes." My voice is a whisper. "It's very okay."

His smile is mostly in his eyes, but it lights up his entire face. "Good."

"I feel like I'm still in that bucket on the pier," I confess. "Still falling."

"Don't worry. I promise I'll catch you."

My pulse is pounding, and the only thing I

want right then is for him to kiss me. So, naturally, I speak.

"Brax..."

"Hmm?" His thumb is still teasing my lip, and I'm pretty sure all of my nerve endings are on fire.

"I think you ought to kiss me now."

"You think so?" His mouth brushes the corner of mine as he speaks, muffling the words.

"I do. In fact I'm certain."

He pulls back enough to hook his finger under my chin. Then he leans in and brushes his lips over mine. A featherlight touch that I feel all the way down to my core.

I hear a soft moaning sound and realize it's coming from me. Then the kiss changes. It's no longer soft and delicate, but hard and demanding and deep. His fingers slide into my hair, holding my head in place as he claims my mouth. His other hand slides down, cupping my breast as our kiss deepens, each of us trying to claim the other, determined to mine every bit of pleasure possible from this moment.

"Brax," I murmur, my mouth pressed to his cheek.

"Hmm?"

I push away so I can see his face. "I feel a

little guilty about kicking you out of your bed last night."

I see the flicker of humor in his eye. He knows exactly where I'm going with this.

"Well, you should. It's a king size bed. Plenty of room to share."

"Exactly what I was thinking," I say. " Sharing is caring."

He presses his hand over his heart. "I'm touched."

I laugh. "Well, not at the moment, but you will be." I slide off the sofa and hold out my hand. "Care to join me in the boudoir?"

He stands, and though I'm being a goof, his expression is nothing but heat. "Yeah," he says. "I'd like that very much."

I hold onto his hand and tug him toward the bedroom, then fall onto the bed while still holding his hand, which forces him to pretty much fall on me, too. He does, and we both end up laughing until I manage to squirm out from under him, then straddle him as soon as he slides all the way up the mattress.

"Definitely more comfortable than the sofa," he says.

"Then let's get you even more cozy." I cup him through the soft material, and he closes his eyes, his low sigh of pleasure familiar even after all these years. But when I untie his sweats and start to tug them down, he opens his eyes and puts his hand over mine.

I tilt my head up to meet his eyes, my expression a question mark.

"I'm sorry," he says. "I know this sounds crazy, but it feels like I'm cheating on Brina."

I swallow, trying to clear the tears that have suddenly gathered in my throat. Then I lean forward until I can brush a kiss over his lips. "I think that's about the sweetest thing I ever heard. But I promise you it's not cheating."

"Because she's dead." His voice is flat. Harsh.

"No. Because she wouldn't want you to spend your life in a damn chastity belt. And because she wouldn't want you to spend your life alone, any more than she'd want you to hide away in some mental dungeon, punishing yourself by refusing to even have fun. On the contrary, she'd want you to live your life. She'd want you to be happy."

"Would she?"

I can't tell if he's asking me or teasing me, but I answer seriously. "I promise. That's what she'd want." I brush some of his sun-kissed hair off his forehead. "We're not making a commitment. We're not planning a future. We're just attracted to each other. We're just exploring. Having fun. That's okay, Brax. Don't over analyze it. The bottom line is that I like you. You make me laugh, and right now, I want you. But if you don't want me … I mean, if you're too confused, then—"

My next sound isn't a word, but a squeal, because he's pulled me to him, his mouth claiming mine as he rolls us both over until he's on top of me, our kiss wild. Ferocious.

This is how I remember him. These are the kisses and touches that come back to me in dreams.

This is what I fantasize about when I go to bed alone at night. Not just the touch, but the connection. Not just pleasure, but the electricity that seems to arc between us, as if we're atomic particles that should never have been separated.

This is why his betrayal hurt so deep.

And it's why I never fully believed it—not really—even after Lambert showed me the proof.

"Samantha," he murmurs, flipping us over so that it's him straddling me. I cup his neck and pull him down, craving his mouth and the claiming way he kisses me. He doesn't protest, and soon his weight is pressing me against the mattress as our mouths collide in such wild, deep kisses that I think I'd be satisfied even if this is all we do tonight.

Except I really hope it won't be all we do tonight.

"Brax," I murmur as I slid my hands down to find the tie of his sweats again. I tug on it, undoing the bow and loosening the waistband. Then I slide my hands inside, my palms cupping the warm skin of his seriously tight ass.

He rises up, breaking the kiss, and I whimper in protest. His mouth curves into a half-smile and he murmurs, "Patience," as he tugs his sweats all the way off, leaving him wearing only the souvenir Tee.

I squirm, tugging at my own shorts, but he takes care of that for me, tugging the legging-style material down until he's pulled the shorts over my feet and has tossed them onto the floor. "Take off the tank," he orders, and I comply immediately, tugging it up and dropping it off the bed. I'm not wearing a bra, and I bite my lower lip as I lay back, my heart pounding as his eyes roam over me. He hasn't seen me in fifteen years, and I suddenly feel as nervous as a Victorian-era bride on her wedding night.

Although that's probably a bit of an exaggeration.

"You're so beautiful," he murmurs.

I laugh, delighted. I love the sentiment, but I also know he can't really see a thing. The light's not on, and the ambient lighting coming through the blinds is minimal.

"Your turn," I say, propping myself up on my elbows. "Off with the shirt."

He complies immediately, tossing it aside with a flourish.

I tilt my head. "Wow. A man who follows orders."

"I'm yours to command," he says. "Tell me what you want."

"You know what I want."

"I want to hear it."

"You," I whisper. "Please, Brax. I want you inside me."

"As you wish." He slides up my body, then makes me melt with a slow, deep kiss. The kind I feel all the way down to my core where his fingers are teasing me, and tiny sparks shoot all through me, the precursor of a coming explosion.

"Please," I beg, spreading my legs. "Please, now."

The words have barely left my lips when he enters me, and I watch his face, his expression a reflection of everything I'm feeling. It's been so long—too long—and I know he isn't going to go slow. I don't want him to. I want hard. I want punishing. I want him to completely own me the way he should have for the last fifteen years. The way he would have if I hadn't screwed up so badly. If I hadn't trusted suspicion but had trusted my heart.

And then thought leaves me and nothing at all matters except the sensations coursing through my body. A wild net of electricity making every one of my cells tingle as all the sparks race toward my core, building and building until the spark morphs into an explosion so intense my body lurches up, shaking, only to be trapped again under Brax as he cries out with his own orgasm. And then, breathing hard, he rolls off me, his hand resting on my belly as his thumb traces patterns in my still-tingling skin.

I sigh, completely content and happier than I can remember being in years. I already want to do it again, and I have to laugh at myself, because I'm desperate to make up for lost time. How had I lived without this? I didn't even realize how alone I felt. Not until I'd showed up at his door. And now, in his bed, I feel whole again.

Group Ultra may have given me solace over the last fifteen years. But it's not my home, even though I accepted it as a substitute.

But Brax...

He's home and hearth combined. He's my life, and he always had been. I was a fool to have ever doubted him, but I was younger then, and clearly more foolish, or I would never have believed what they thought the evidence showed. On the contrary, I would have told him everything, and it would be me—Sabrina—in this bed tonight, and not a woman who doesn't even really exist.

I screwed up back then; I know that now.

And because of that, the man who has always been the center of my life made love with a figment of my imagination tonight.

But that stops now.

We'll have to come up with a plan, of course. I'll talk to Lambert and the senior agents like Jorge. I'll lay it all out, and they'll have to see the truth. We can even top it off with a polygraph. But in the end, they'll bring Brax in, too, and we'll finally be together, just like we should have been so long ago.

Or we could just quit and move to a desert island together. Frankly, I'd be fine with that, too. Or a zillion other options. All I want is to be back in his arms, because the only thing I'm certain of is that now that I have him back, I won't survive if I lose him again.

His fingers stroke my arm as his lips brush the curve of my ear.

"What are you thinking?"

I laugh. "That I never want you to stop."

He chuckles. "Never's a long time. But we can give it a try." He shifts his position, then bends his head again and kisses my navel. Then he trails kisses lower, his lips teasing my lower belly, then going even further as I spread my legs and close my eyes, already half-swept away by the pleasure building inside me.

I'm waxed, and his lips feel glorious against the soft skin of my pubis as he moves lower still, until—

The scar. Oh, god, the scar.

My entire body goes cold, and I start to roll over. But his hands are tight on my hips now, and it's not a sensual touch anymore. My chest tightens, and I want to cry.

I know what this means.

And more than anything in the world, I wish that could press *rewind* and have a do-over of the last fifteen years.

The scar.

His lips brushed over it, and at first he didn't realize what it was. Then he heard her gasp and felt the way her body tensed.

And that's when he knew.

That's when he understood.

She wasn't Samantha. She wasn't even a twin.

She was Sabrina.

She was the woman he'd loved. The woman he'd mourned.

And now he knew she was the woman who betrayed him.

He sat up, then reached for his sweats and tugged them on. Then he stood up, turned around just long enough to give her one long, cold glare, and left the bedroom, pulling the door shut behind him.

The moment he sat on the couch, though, the tension left his body. He wanted to cry like a baby.

All this time...

All this time, he'd believed she was dead. Instead, she'd lied to him. She was alive—vibrantly alive. And yet she'd hidden from him. Kept her distance because she believed—she actually fucking believed—that he had something to do with that goddamn bomb.

Fuck.

He shouldn't have touched her. He should never have let himself fall for "Samantha." For the fiction Sabrina had spun. And why the hell had she let herself get so close? He'd been right there when the thug had attacked her all those years ago. The knife slicing through the thin cotton of her dress and her tender flesh so fast that Brax hadn't even had time to react.

She'd been so young, and so perfect. And the prick had got away, because Brax couldn't leave her. On the contrary, he'd flagged down a cop—and that was risky enough—who'd taken them to the nearest emergency room. She'd gotten stitched up, and while the cop was waiting for the triage team to finish so he could talk to her, they'd slipped out through a connecting room, waited it out in a supply closet, then finally disappeared back into the night.

It had taken over a month before he could touch her again, and when the red of the scar finally faded, she called it her badge of honor. Points toward starting her own street gang.

He'd been so proud of her for owning it, and he wondered how the hell she could have forgotten about it.

Except he didn't. Not really. He'd been lost in the moment, too. And he didn't doubt at all that her desire was real.

She still wanted him; that much was for sure.

But after the way she betrayed him? Well, she may still want him, but he didn't want her at all.

That, at least, was what he told himself.

He stayed on the sofa, dozing as he waited for her to come out of the bedroom. To toss bullshit explanations his way. But she didn't come, and soon enough the room started to fade, and it was only when the sun streamed in through the kitchen that he blinked his way back to consciousness.

The door to the bedroom was cracked, and

he crossed to it and peeked in, expecting to find her gone.

But there she was, sitting on the edge of the bed, her eyes swollen.

"Will it even matter if I say I'm sorry?"

"No."

She licked her lips, nodding slowly. "I don't blame you. But I'm going to say it anyway. I'm sorry. So very, very sorry."

"And you think that makes up for it?" He heard the steel in his voice and wished that anger could cause physical pain. God knew he suffered enough believing she was dead.

"Tell me," he demanded. "Tell me what you planned. Why you faked your death. And why you ran from me after spending years telling me you loved me."

"I did." She licked her lips. "I still do."

"Don't. Don't say that."

She hung her head, nodding almost imperceptibly. "I had a warning," she said. "I told you about it, remember? That I had a bad feeling. That I wanted to just leave—to run away with you. But you said I just had jitters. Then you got out of the car to go to the relay point."

She waited for him to say something, and when he didn't, she drew a breath and continued. "I didn't want to believe the threat was real, but they told me there was a bomb in the van. They told me you were working with Darrin. That the two of you wanted to thin the team so you could have a bigger share. And—and that I was expendable."

"You believed that?" His voice felt like ice.

"I didn't know what to believe, but no. I didn't. Not at first." She licked her lips. "But then you didn't come back right away. You just stayed there, away from the van. And I started to get nervous. And then there was Jorge, racing toward my door. And he yanked it open and pulled me out." She closed her eyes and took a deep breath. "And that's when the car exploded.

"Jorge saved me," she continued. "And there really was a bomb. And you really stayed away. You ignored my worries and you stayed away. So what the hell was I supposed to think?"

"That I loved you, dammit."

Tears spilled from her eyes. "They showed me photos. You by the van. You looking up into the tire well. They said you were checking the bomb."

"I never—fuck, Brina. They faked them. And you believed them over me."

She nodded, looking miserable. "I didn't

want to, but what else made sense? Especially since you were gone. Just *poof.*"

"I was supposed to hang around like some damn Judas Goat?"

"If you were innocent, yes." Her voice rose in pitch. "Maybe not for them, but you could have gotten word to me."

"You were dead," he snapped. "I was a broken fucking hull of a man and I thought you were dead. How the fuck was I supposed to get you a message?"

She didn't answer. Just drew in a long breath, then released it. "For about a year, I hated you. I didn't understand how you could do that to me. And to do it for money, when we'd turned down so many jobs that would have paid great because they were too risky and we knew one or both of us might get hurt. But then there was this. It was baffling, and I was so, so angry."

She sat up straighter. "But then they gave me a job, and I threw myself into it."

"Who?"

"A government organization. That's all I can tell you. Jorge got me an interview with the director. And once I was in, I had access to a lot of resources. I started poking around, trying to find you. I told myself it was for revenge, but that wasn't true. Not really. I wanted answers. I wanted to hear it straight from you why you would do that to me."

"I didn't," he growled.

"Back then, I didn't believe that."

"Back then?"

"For about two years. I was hurt and scared and young. And then I started to wonder. I don't remember what changed, but it did. I missed you, but it was more than that. But there was no Braxton Reed out there. Not one who was under the age of sixty. So I thought that either meant you were dead or that you really had planted the bomb, and didn't want to use a tainted name that we'd chosen together."

"I didn't use it at first because of you. It was too painful. You were dead, after all."

"But later you did."

He nodded. "When I entered the FBI Academy. They knew about my entire past, and I told them we'd already put the paper work in place." He shrugged. "So that's when I became Brax."

"I ran a search about every six months. That name and all the others on our list. At first I only found the record we set up. But then I finally found more. Credit cards and tax returns and a drivers license. So I found you after all."

"And you came here as your twin sister to what? Punish me?"

She licked her lips. "I wanted to learn the truth. I wanted to learn that you didn't really do that to me."

"I didn't."

"I believe you," she said. "And I'm sorry. Please, Brax. Can't you understand? Can't you forgive me?"

But all he could do was look her in the eye, shake his head, and say, very simply, *"No."*

For a moment she just sat there. Then she nodded. "I'll get my stuff and go."

"No." The force and speed of the protest surprised him. "We're in the middle of a job. They think we're a couple. We're not changing a damn thing. Except that I'm not touching you again except for show, and then only when it's absolutely necessary."

She bit her lower lip, then whispered, "I understand."

"You can sleep on the couch," he said. Then he stood and went back to his bedroom, shutting the door. And then, just so she'd hear the click, he locked it, too.

He didn't sleep. How could he? He was too damn broken. So when his alarm chimed at eight, he got up and stumbled out of the bedroom to make coffee.

She was gone. All that remained was a note saying that she had to go to work, but so long as he intended to keep up the pretense, she'd be back.

The worst part was that she signed the note, *Love, Brina.*

He crumpled it up, then threw it away.

CHAPTER FIFTEEN

B rax had already called Ryan to set up an early-morning meeting, and he was throwing on a suit when the doorbell chimed. He muttered a curse—he was already later than he'd intended, and he had no interest in dealing with his landlord or someone looking to sell him something at the moment.

He ignored the chime, finished getting dressed, then headed into his living room.

Then stopped when he saw the woman sipping coffee by his breakfast bar.

"What the fuck, Cami? Don't you knock?"

"Don't you answer?"

"Right. Sorry." He drew a breath as he made a beeline for the coffee pot. "I'm a little bit frazzled."

She looked him up and down. "No shit. Want me to frazzle you some more?"

He'd been pouring with his back to her. Now he turned, concerned by something in the tone of her voice. "What's going on?"

"Oh, not much. Just that your new girlfriend happens to also be your old one."

"Yeah," he said after a beat. "I know."

Her eyes widened. "Why didn't you tell me?"

"Because I found out last night. In bed."

"She told you?"

"She did not." He heard the coldness in his voice. From Cami's expression, she'd heard it, too.

"Dare I ask?"

"She has a scar. An intimate scar. And while I didn't calculate the odds, I didn't think it was likely that her twin would have it, too."

"Holy shit." Cami climbed onto one of the bar stools, then took a long slug of coffee, something she often did when she wanted a conversational gap with sufficient thinking time built in. "So that was a surprise for you, I'm guessing."

"Yeah," he said dryly. "You could say that."

"I'm really sorry. Is she here?"

"She's gone."

"Is she coming back?"

"I don't know," he said, which was the absolute truth. "I don't care." That one was more of a fiction. But once enough time passed, she'd be out of his system. It would be a true enough statement then.

He focused his attention on Cami. "What does it matter? Actually, back up. How did you find out she's really Sabrina?"

Cami held up the plastic water bottle she often carried throughout the day. "I handed it to her. She didn't even think twice. And, *bingo*, fingerprints."

"Smart," he said. Contrary to many folks' belief, identical twins weren't entirely identical. At the very least, their fingerprints were unique.

"I came over because I was worried. She's pretending to be a non-existent sister because otherwise she has to stay hidden. She's dead, right?"

"Apparently not."

"Good point, but you know what I mean. But the question is why? Why fake her death? Or if she didn't fake it and managed to somehow escape the bomb, why come out of hiding after so many years, only to get involved with a man who investigates shit like that for a living."

"I have no idea. I'm not sure I care."

She stared him down. Cami never had been one to take his bullshit.

"Yeah, you do," she said.

"Fine. I do. I care. But only because I'm curious. I'm wiping my hands of that woman."

Cami kept her eyes on his face as she finished the last of her coffee. "She hurt you that much?"

He didn't answer.

"I'm sorry," she said. "I know you love her."

"Loved. Many, many years ago."

Cami just shook her head. "My grammar is just fine. I used exactly the right tense. And," she said, holding up a hand to cut him off, "you need to tell Ryan. Like right now. She's one of the original members of the heist team. I'm thinking that can't be good."

"I know. I'm on my way in right now. Mason needs to know, too. Not only about Sabrina, but that we're most likely shifting the plan to run the heist while the diamond's in transit. And," he added, "we'll want to switch the actual Sisters with the counterfeit as soon as possible. If they heist succeeds, they still won't have shit.

"I'll go in with you. I'm on the heist team. He might want me in the meeting. Especially since Sabrina knows about the plan. We may have to change it again."

"We should," she said. "After all—"

The sharp ring of Brax's cell phone interrupted her, and he snatched it up, frowning when he saw that the call was from Ryan.

"Am I late? I thought we said nine," he said.

"We did," Ryan said. "But things have changed. Get here as soon as you can and come straight to my office."

"Of course. Cami, too?" He had the call on speaker, and realized when Ryan hesitated, that perhaps he should have taken it privately.

"No," Ryan said. "For now, it's just you."

"Of course," he said, then turned to Cami after they ended the call.

"What the fuck?" she said.

Brax could only shake his head.

"Sorry. Traffic was a nightmare," Brax said, pushing through the door into Ryan's office. "What the fuck's going on that Cami can't know about it?"

Behind the desk, Ryan lifted an eyebrow.

ENTWINED WITH YOU   231

"Sorry," Brax said. "I just had a shitty night."

"I'm afraid I'm about to do the same for your day," Ryan said.

Brax pinched the bridge of his nose. "Why am I not surprised?" Honestly, his karma just kept spiraling down…

"Have a seat," Ryan said, then pushed a button on his desktop console. Immediately, the whiteboard on the far side of Ryan's office slid up, revealing a black screen with the SSA logo. He pressed another button, and the room filled with an electronic hiss. Then the screen disappeared and the face of Colonel Anderson Seagrave—along with the wall of his office lined with various military and governmental commendations and accolades—appeared on screen.

Ryan tapped something into the system, and Seagrave's image slid to one side and another video box popped up. Brax didn't recognize the man in the image, but he wasn't in an office. He looked to be sitting at a desk in a bedroom, if the unmade bed behind him was any indication.

"Agent Reed," the colonel said.

"Sir."

"We're joined by Morris Grey. Are you familiar with each other?"

"I've read Agent Reed's file," Grey said, making Brax frown. Who was this guy, and why was he poking his nose into Brax's personal information?

"I'm afraid I haven't had the pleasure," Brax said, with more heat than was probably politic, but under the circumstances, he felt justified.

If the slight grin he saw on Seagrave's face was any indication, Brax's irritation was showing.

"Pleasure to meet you," he said grudgingly.

"Likewise," Grey said.

"Agent Grey is one of our best operatives at the SOC. He's particularly good at undercover work. Has a knack for blending in.

Brax just nodded, not at all sure where this was going.

"He's currently on assignment. Undercover at Group Ultra.

"Oh," Brax said, perking up.

"He's not been in place long, so he hasn't gained enough trust from his supervisors to be as useful as we anticipate. But what he does have are eyes and an incredible memory for faces. And we, of course, have excellent artists on staff."

Brax forced himself not to urge Seagrave to cut to the chase. Even though he really just wanted to cut to the chase. Because right then, Brax didn't have an inkling of what Grey could have seen that had anything to do with him.

"Police sketches," Seagrave said, as if reading Brax's mind and answering him. "These three sketches might be of some interest to you."

Seagrave and Grey disappeared from the screen, replaced by a composite sketch of a fifty-something man with unruly hair, a strong jaw, and large eyes that seemed to look out through the monitor.

"Killion Lambert," announced Seagrave's disembodied voice. "The director of Group Ultra, and someone for whom we didn't yet have any identifying material."

"Good job, Grey," Brax said, and he genuinely meant it.

"Do you recognize this man?" Seagrave asked.

The image now on the screen had a thin face, wavy hair cut short, a full mouth, and eyebrows that were almost flat. There was something familiar about him, but—

"Jorge Ramos," Seagrave said at the same time the name popped into Brax's mind.

"Are you going to tell me he's also at Group Ultra?"

"Correct," Seagrave said. "And we have reason to believe he's been an operative there for almost two decades."

"He was part of the original team to steal the Sisters," Brax said, although both Ryan and Seagrave undoubtedly knew that. "If you're right, he was with Group Ultra when Sabrina's van exploded."

"That's correct," Seagrave said. He didn't elaborate. Instead, he said, "And this is the final sketch."

The screen went to static for a bit before coming into focus. When it did, Brax gasped. This time, the sketch was of a woman.

Sabrina.

"No," he said. "Absolutely not. There is no way in hell she'd be part of a group like that. It's not even debatable."

"And yet there she is."

"No. I don't believe it."

"We have reason to believe she's been duped," Ryan said gently. "From what we've learned, most of their lower-and mid-level agents have been. They believe they're working for a covert branch of the SOC. Obviously, they're not. Lambert clearly knows the real score. Ramos is a question mark. Samantha, we believe, is an innocent."

"Fuck," Brax said. "Is she there now?"

"We believe so. We don't have confirmation."

"Shit. Shit, shit, *shit.*" He held up a hand, apologizing to the man on the screen and the man behind the desk. And debating whether or not to tell these two men who "Samantha" really was.

He didn't want to. Doing that would only rip down whatever tiny bit of trust still existed between them. But there were much bigger things at play than his relationship with Brina.

Now, however, probably wasn't the time.

He drew in a tight breath. "We know the SOC's shadow is trying to steal the sisters. I doubt it's because Lambert wants to decorate his living room. Do we know why they need those diamonds?"

"We don't," Ryan says.

"Actually, we do," Seagrave corrected. "Agent Grey?"

"Lambert briefed us," Grey said. "According

to him, there's a terrorist group looking to steal the Sisters because a diamond of their size and quality is needed to power some James Bond style space laser."

"Really." Ryan's brows rose. "I have to admit that's the first time I've heard that one."

"I'm afraid it's legit," Seagrave said. "If that's truly their purpose, we can't risk them getting those diamonds."

"Jorge knows that we're planning on planting the counterfeit diamond in Wolfe's vault," Brax said. "Odds are good, if he's a higher level at Group Ultra, then he knows he needs to send in a team before we make the switch. And since the heist team is meeting later today, that means that ideally those diamonds will be in the clear in the next few hours. How the hell are we going to make that happen?"

"I can take care of that," Ryan said.

"How?" Seagrave asked.

"I apologize, Morris, but this is need-to-know only. I'm blacking you out."

"Understood, sir."

Brax waited, expecting Ryan to ask him to step out of the room. Instead, Ryan just shook his head. "You're the head of Omega Team," he reminded Brax. "You need to know."

"Yes, sir."

"What time is the heist team meeting?"

"Seven."

"Perfect. Plan it out however you want then fill me in. I'll keep Wolfe in the loop. Don't worry. The real Sisters will be out of the Wolfe home within the next two hours and they'll stay out until after the gala."

"How? And where are they going?"

"Damien's house. It's not common knowledge, but there's a vault beneath it. No one's getting in there to get the Sisters."

"But how are you getting them there?"

"Trisha—Wolfe's wife—is about to get an invitation from Nikki to come over for lunch. I have a feeling she'll accept."

Brax chuckled. "Fair enough. I'll wipe that worry out of my head. And I'll try to get a read on Jorge at the meeting this afternoon. We'll plan to run a few rehearsals between now and the gala, too, just to keep up the show."

Ryan turned Grey's sound and visual back on. "Sorry about that. We're just about done here."

"Of course. Not a problem."

"Final order of business," Ryan said. "We're bringing Sabrina in. Morris, you're an excellent asset. But you're not a field agent. And we could use a double."

"Sir," Brax began, "I don't know..."

"It's not your call. I'm telling you only as a courtesy. And because I want you to set up the meet."

"Sir?"

"Ask her to come to your office for lunch today. Bring her through from Z-Tech to one of the conference rooms. I'll join you a few minutes in. As for you, Grey, I don't think you should be at that meeting, but if Colonel Seagrave agrees, I'd like you to arrange a time to talk with her sometime after. Perhaps a coffee after work. She may well want to vent to someone else who's straddling these two organizations."

"Yes, sir. I'd be happy to."

Brax dragged his fingers through his hair. "I really don't think—"

"Agent Reed," Ryan said gently. "She needs to know the truth. And from what I've read and seen, she has solid skills. And it's not just about recruiting her to SSA. She needs to know the situation she's in."

He wanted to curse. Hell, he wanted to throw something.

Unfortunately, Ryan was right.

"I'll get her in. We had—we had sort of a fight. But I'll call her. I'll get her here."

Ryan nodded. "And then we'll go from there."

CHAPTER SIXTEEN

I end the call with Brax, positively giddy that
he wants to talk. I know I hurt him. Even if
I was justified in running after the bombing,
that doesn't matter. I still hate myself for ever
believing he could have tried to kill me.

And if I hate myself for it, then can I really
blame him for feeling the same way?

Except that's not even the deepest cut. No, I
sliced even deeper when I returned years later
after I'd had the luxury of oodles of time in
which to gather myself. To think. To let everything I knew settle in my heart.

If I'd done that, I would have known with
unerring certainty that Brax would never hurt
me. Even right now, today, after knowing that
I've once again twisted the knife, I'm certain

that I can always count on him to help when I'm in danger or trouble.

That's because he loves me.

But I didn't look at the love. I looked at my own fear, and even as my fear faded, I still nurtured the doubts because everyone around me said I should. I wasn't Sabrina anymore, they reminded me. I was Samantha. Sabrina was dead.

She was dead because someone had killed her. And they told me that someone was him.

Deep down, I've always known that he had nothing to do with the bombing. It's simply impossible. I know him. And he would never hurt me. That's simply not who he is.

But I let fear block both reason and love. And in doing so, I hurt the man I care most about. A man who truly loves me, and who I wounded so deeply that I was certain he'd never forgive me.

But then he called...

I smile, reliving the pleasure of seeing his name pop up on my phone screen, then hearing his voice. He called, and my entire day turned bright.

I hope he forgives me.

I hope he still loves me.

But if he doesn't, I know it's only myself I have to blame.

———

Z-Tech Data Processing is housed in a nondescript building in Santa Monica. To be honest, it's not the kind place I would have ever expected Brax to work, but at the same time, considering all the adventures we had in our youth, maybe he was thrilled to finally settle down to something tame.

I pull open the glass door, then step inside. A young woman who's probably barely twenty smiles at me from behind a counter adorned with the Z-Tech logo. "Can I help you?"

"I'm meeting Braxton Reed. I'm not sure where I'm supposed to go."

"Let me check that for you." She taps on her keypad, then looks back at me, her ultra-white smile practically glowing under the fluorescent lights. "It looks like he reserved a conference room. If you'll follow me?"

She puts a little *Please Wait* sign on the counter, the leads me through a maze of workstations to a door at the back. We go through, take a service elevator down, then walk to the end of a long hallway until I find myself standing in front of a wood-paneled door labeled *Conference Room C*.

She opens the door and ushers me in. "He'll be right with you."

Then she's gone and I'm all alone in a huge conference room with four long tables set up to form a square. A huge whiteboard hangs on one wall. And I'm struck with the perverse thought that he's going to use a variety of colorful dry erase markers to demonstrate exactly how much I hurt him.

Oh, please no.

I'm just about to take a seat when I hear the door open. I spin around, and there he is, tall and lean and dressed in a suit, and looking as comfortable in that as he does in jeans. That's one of his gifts—something we used shamelessly on the grift. The man can pull off any outfit.

"Thanks for coming," he says, his long strides eating up the yards between us.

"Brax, I'm so sorry about—well, about every-thing. I should have trusted you from the very beginning. I knew better. I knew *you*. But I was scared and confused and everyone was talking at me and you were gone."

I swallow then blink back tears. "I listened

to them instead of listening to me, and if you don't forgive me, I think I'll hate myself for that for the rest of my life."

His mouth curves into a smile. "Well, we can't have that."

It takes me a minute to process the fact that his smile is tender, his eyes are soft. And when he takes my hand and gently kisses my fingertips, I burst into tears.

"Hey," he says, pulling me close. "Come on, baby. That wasn't the reaction I was looking for."

I manage to make some sort of affirmative movement with my head, but there tears are still flowing. Not because of what he said, but because of what he didn't say. Understanding. Forgiveness.

Love.

I draw a deep breath, then step back. When I do, my tears turn to giggles. "Sorry! Sorry! It's just—oh, hell, Brax. I made a complete mess of your suit."

He glances down at the tear-stained material that, if we're being honest, is probably a little snot-stained now, too. "It's not a problem. You can cry on my clothes anytime you wish. Hopefully the next time you do, it won't be because I hurt you."

I blink. "You didn't hurt me. I'm the one who walked away. Who didn't trust you. I should never have—"

He cuts me off with a finger to my lips. "I propose a truce. You didn't hurt me, and I didn't hurt you. And the next time one of us doesn't hurt the other, we'll sit down on the couch with a glass of wine or whiskey and either talk it through or get wasted and roll around naked until we forget what the problem even was."

I'm fighting to hold back another round of tears. "I love you."

"Never stop saying that."

"I won't."

"And will you do one other thing for me?"

I nod.

"Will you trust me. No matter how crazy something might seem, will you trust me that I'm doing the right thing? Will you trust that I won't ever lie to you?"

"Yes," I say, flinging myself at him, my arms going around his waist as I hold him close, never wanting to let go. But I do, of course. Eventually I step back, glance around the mostly bare room

for a box of tissues, then dig in my purse for a
crumpled one when my search comes up empty.

"Brax?" I ask, my eyes sweeping the room
again. "Why are we having this conversation in
here?"

"I need to tell you something. I thought it
would be easier in a conference room." His
voice is calm and level. Eerily calm and level.

"Because of the visual aids?"

I was being sarcastic, but he just nods and
says, "Yes."

"Oh. Okay. Should I sit down. Because I
kind of want to. To be honest, you're freaking
me out a little."

"I know. I'm sorry." I've pulled out a chair to
sit in, but he's perched on the table beside me. "I
have a few things to tell you. You won't like it.
But I need you to listen. Can you do that?"

He's still speaking in that eerie calm, and
I'm certain that's the freakiest part of this entire
situation.

I'm wrong.

Twenty minutes later I'm sitting numb in
my chair, having been battered with words like
*manipulation, enemy of the state, crimes against
the state, unsanctioned missions, high-level
conspiracies,* and on and on and on.

"You can't be serious. That's the stuff of Hollywood, not real life."

He shakes his head. "On the contrary, it's about as real as it gets. The Sisters, for example. That supposed laser weapon that Group Ultra is trying to prevent going active by protecting those diamonds?"

I nod, still numb.

"They're not trying to keep the diamonds from that weapon. They're trying to gain control of the weapon."

"You're sure?" I can tell from his face that he's sure. And when he turns on the giant screen, then scrolls through some slides he's preloaded to his phone, I see just how deep this monster he's talking about goes.

I bolt to my feet. "I think I'm going to be sick." I start to run toward the door, then stop, just letting the waves of nausea pass over me as a truly vile thought enters my mind. "Am I in trouble?"

"No, baby. No. You're here because we need your help."

He presses a button and tells the woman who responds that he's ready for Ryan. A few minutes later, a gorgeous and familiar-looking man steps in. "You're Jamie Hunter's husband,"

I blurt, then blush like an idiot. Now really isn't the time.

He only laughs. "I'm surprised you even noticed me in whatever photo you saw. Most people only see Jamie."

"Can you blame them?" His wife is a stunning actress whom the camera absolutely loves.

"How are you holding up?" Ryan asks. "Did Brax fill you in?"

"He filled me in, yes," I say, reaching for his hand. I immediately regret doing that; it's probably not cool to hold hands in front of his boss. But Brax takes mine immediately and gives it a soft squeeze.

"As for holding up," I continue. "The jury's still out."

"Well, here's where I ask you the big question. We're trying to bring this organization and all it's cells down. That's a big job, and not one that can be done overnight. We need people on the inside. Right now, in LA, we only have one." He meets my eyes. "We'd like to have two."

I try to answer, but my mouth has gone dry. I try again. "Who's already in?"

Ryan and Brax exchange a glance, then Ryan nods. "Morris Grey."

"Oh," I say, suddenly understanding why he asked if I wanted to meet for a drink tomorrow.

"I won't sugar coat it. The job's dangerous. But it's also important. And if you go in, Brax has agreed to join."

I frown. "Doing data entry?"

Ryan laughs. "No. That's a cover. Brax is one of our purely covert agents. Outside the office, there's no hint of what he does for Stark Security.

"Stark Security," I repeat, recalling a time when Director Lambert had told a small group of us that Damien Stark's spin-off security company was a well-known front for money laundering and drug trafficking. The though must show on my face, because Brax tells me it's not true.

I tilt my head up to him, and though I don't say it aloud, I know he understands me. *How the hell am I supposed to know what's true?*

He doesn't answer. But in his silence I hear the promise I already made. That I would always trust him.

And so that's that. I draw a breath, look between the two men, and simply ask, "So what do I do now?"

CHAPTER SEVENTEEN

As it turns out, the answer to "what do I do now," is pretty simple: business as usual. Except now I'm focusing on remembering details so that I can pass them back to Stark Security and the real SOC. I can't say I love the job—it's stressful as shit—but at the same time, it's not that different than what was doing before. Now I'm just doing it with eyes wide open. And my true boss doesn't even work in the building.

"This is strange," I say after my second day in my new role. "Living a double-life, I mean. But it's not as strange as I thought it would be."

"That's because you've been doing it all your life," Brax says, rubbing my feet that I've plunked on his lap.

We're on the sofa in his apartment, which, as of yesterday, is officially *our* apartment. Though we're going to have to move more of my stuff over for it to really feel like mine.

I consider what he said. "You may be right. I never felt like I was living a double-life before, though. It was just the job. Survival. It was be whoever you had to be to get from one moment to the next."

"The same, but different," he says. "But either way, I think we're uniquely well-suited for the work."

"Good," I say. I pull my legs up under me and scoot closer so I'm leaning against him. "I like working with you again. I like being us again."

"Me, too," he says, as I shift again, this time to straddle him. "I have some interesting information already," I say.

"Yeah? What's that?"

"I have over an hour before I'm supposed to meet Morris at Clandestine." I wiggle a little more, the invitation obvious. "However will we pass the time?"

"My mind's a complete blank," he says, as his fingers find the button of my jeans.

"Mine too," I say, as my fingers go to work

on the buttons of his shirt. "Maybe we should—oh!" I squeal with laughter, then hook my legs around his waist as he somehow manages to rise with me attached to him, arms and legs holding tight.

He carries me the short distance to the bedroom, tosses me onto the mattress, then joins me there.

"Want me to tell you what I have planned?"

"Nope," I say, sliding his shirt off. "Why don't you just show me?"

It's a brilliant suggestion if I do say so myself, though to be perfectly accurate, it wasn't *show* so much as *feel*. Because what Brax had me do was stretch out on the bed with my eyes closed as he proceeded to kiss and stroke and undress every single part of my body.

Every.

Single.

Part.

Honestly, I'm so relaxed when the timer I set goes off that I want to text Morris that we'll grab our drink tomorrow.

Which I would. Except this isn't just a drink. This is our How We Handle Being The Two Double Agents at Group Ultra chat.

That's why I force myself to my feet with a

sigh of pleasure coupled with a groan of annoyance.

"I really wish I was staying," I tell Brax, who's stretched out naked on top of the bed covers.

"So do I," he says.

"Hold that thought. The bar's only twenty minutes away. Another twenty for a drink and our chat, and twenty back home. An hour. Tops. I'll try to make it in fifty-two minutes.

He grins, taps the button on his watch to start the timer, and says, "Go."

I roll my eyes, race through finishing getting dressed, then sprint down to my car.

I actually make it to the bar—uninspiringly named *Joe's*—in seventeen minutes.

Clearly, it's shaping up to be a stellar day.

I wave to the owner, and since I don't see Morris, I head to the back to hit the rest room before grabbing us a table. There's only the one, and while the doorknob turns, the door itself is stuck.

I frown, then put my shoulder against the door and push until it's open enough for me to barely squeeze through.

I get my head in, then look down to see what the obstruction is.

It's Morris.

I scream and jerk back automatically, banging my skull in the process.

I pull out my phone and dial 911, then push through the exit to the alley just so I can get some air.

I don't even have a chance to draw a breath before someone tall and strong hits me over the head, knocks my phone from my hand, and the rest of the world goes completely black.

Brax stared at the body on the floor of the bathroom stall. Morris Grey had been tortured before he'd been killed. Somebody had locked themselves in the one-hole bathroom and spent his time making sure Morris had a long, long night filled with nothing but pain.

He wondered what Grey had given up. If Group Ultra now knew that Sabrina was working with Stark Security and the SOC.

Of course they did. That's why they'd taken her.

And that's why they would kill her once they squeezed every bit of intel out of her.

They had to hurry. Dear god, they had to hurry.

Nausea rose, and he forced it down. Physical aches, regrets, should-haves. All of those were useless now. All that mattered—all that he could permit himself to focus on—was getting her back. Locating her. Getting to her. Setting her free.

And then holding her tight until he was certain she was real and safe and alive.

"We'll get her back," Mason said, standing beside him and looking down at the corpse with an expression that was both determined and sad.

"We will," Brax said, because no other option was possible.

His phone rang, and he snatched it up eagerly, a tiny sprig of hope blooming when he saw that the call was from Quincy. "Tell me," he said, without preamble.

"Found him," Quincy said. "I'm about to settle in for a nice long chat with him."

"Just don't make it too long. We don't have much time. *She* doesn't have much time."

"If he knows where she is, I'll get it out of him," Quincy promised. "And I'll get it fast."

"Call me when you have something."

"You know I will," Quincy said, then ended the call.

Brax and Mason were at Joe's, the bar where Sabrina had been going to meet Morris Grey. Apparently she'd found Grey's body—and then she'd been taken. Now the only sign of her was her phone that had been left in the alley behind the bar.

Quincy Radcliffe was working with them. Former MI-6, Quincy had been with Stark Security almost from the beginning. And while he had mad skills in everything from weapons to hand-to-hand, his true genius was extracting information. *Oh, yes.* They'd find her.

But first they had to get the information out of Jorge Ramos, the little Group Ultra worm who had not only doctored the photos that supposedly showed Brax rigging Sabrina's van, but had suggested to Lambert that he recruit Sabrina all those years ago.

As soon as Brax learned that Sabrina had been taken, the entirety of the SSA had burst into action. Not fast enough, though. Lambert was gone, presumably out of the country. A few low-level operatives remained on site, and were being processed by the SOC. Seagrave himself was interviewing each one to learn if they had

any information at all about Sabrina's where-
abouts. So far, his status updates over the last
ninety minutes had all been negative.

Brax had originally urged Seagrave to cage
the fuckers, but Quincy had suggested otherwise. "They're ants, and ants always head to the
Queen. Put tails on them. Tap their phones.
Use whatever tricks we have. It might take
years, but if we watch the workers, eventually
we'll find Lambert. Not to mention the heads of
the other cells."

It was good advice, and Seagrave took it,
releasing each of the office drones after their exit
interview, and assuring that a SOC agent was
monitoring.

Brax's phone rang. *Quincy.*

"Tell me you got Jorge. And that he's given
you something."

"Fuck you," a gravely voice said. Not
Quincy. *Jorge.*

"Where is she?"

"Go to hell, fucker."

"He's on something," Quincy said, coming
on the line. "The little bastard's trying to cooperate, believe it or not, but his brain's too fried
from whatever was already in his system before
we started this interrogation. Drug interactions.

Sorry. He seemed clean, and we didn't have time for a blood test."

"Bitch is gonna burn." The words were soft in the background, but Brax could make them out, and they made his stomach twist in fear. "Gonna burn in hell, hell, the devil's own hell."

Brax had no idea where they'd taken Sabrina. But he knew they had to find out fast.

Because what Jorge Ramos was telling them was that wherever she was hidden, that place was about to go up in flames.

CHAPTER EIGHTEEN

I am not going to die today. And I am definitely not going to burn to death. I already escaped that fate once when I bolted from a rigged van. I'm not going to come full circle to die inside a warehouse when it goes up in flames.

That's my plan, at least. My problem is that Jorge had something else in mind. And that's why I'm currently tied to a post in a warehouse in god knows where, and the stacks of cardboard and newspapers in all the corners are already starting to catch from the bits of crumpled newspaper and strips of cloth he set around the perimeter before telling that he needed to get home, but that he'd see me tomorrow.

Or, at least, he'd see my ashes.

How the hell could I have once believed he was a friend?

I cough from the increasing smoke, then force myself to keep scraping at my bonds. My upper arms ache, but my wrists are lashed together behind my back and the post I'm leaning against. I'm trying to rub the tape that's binding my wrist along the post to cut it, but so far, I'm having no luck. None that I can tell anyway. It's not as if I can see if I'm making progress.

Think, dammit, think.

But I am thinking. And there's nothing else I can do. I'm literally tied to a post surrounded by a slow but growing fire.

Before he left, Jorge had said he was executing me in a fine tradition of burning witches. "Oh, did I say *witches?* I meant *bitches.*"

I would have flipped him the finger, but my hands were tied.

I really don't want to die here.

And I'm not going to. I'm not. I may be stuck, but Brax is looking for me, I'm certain of it. Brax and all of Stark Security and the SOC. They're not going to give up, I know they won't.

I'm not giving up either, but it's getting

harder and harder to breathe, and while I'm certain Brax will find me, I hope the Powers that Be realize that my wish is to be found alive. Not as a pile of ash.

Just pointing that out in case anyone out there is listening.

I'm getting giddy. Light-headed.

It's the smoke.

I tilt my head down, remembering all the elementary school lessons about staying low. I even try to slide down the pole, and am surprised when my bound wrists are permitted to move that direction.

It's just a few feet, but the schools got it right. It's easier to breathe down here. Not by much, but at this point, I'll take anything someone throws at me. Except a ball of flame.

Yeah. Giddy.

Dammit, Sabrina. Focus. Stay sharp.

Yes. Sharp. I have to stay—

My eye lands on a chip of concrete from the floor. It's roughly the shape of a triangle, and if I can just get my foot to draw it over, then maybe —just maybe—I can circle around the post and reach it with my fingers.

I might end up accidentally slicing my

wrists. But on the other hand, maybe I'll manage to saw through this tape.

Considering how fast the papers are starting to burn now, I don't have a choice. I'm fresh out of time and running out of air.

And I really, really don't want to die.

"Break it down," Brax shouted, throwing himself at the door. "She's in there. She's got to be. *Break it the fuck down.*"

"It's not budging."

Mason was beside him, trying to get through the door of the burning warehouse on the outskirts of town. They'd heard about it on the radio—a fire at an abandoned warehouse and no firetrucks responding as all crews were occupied with a massive apartment fire.

Jorge had trapped her in there. Then he started the fire and tried to get away. Quincy's team had caught him, but he'd held onto his secret, refusing to reveal where he'd stashed Sabrina.

But that news report had led them here, and there was still time. She was alive in there. She had to be, because he couldn't let himself consider any other reality.

"This is taking too long," Mason said.

"Fuck it. We're idiots." Brax raced back to Old Blue. He loved that car, but it would be worth it if the thing could break that door down. He prayed it could.

His next car would be an SUV.

He started the car, revved the engine, then floored it, desperately hoping she wasn't sprawled on the ground in front of the floor. But the car was flying now and he had to risk it, because whether by car or asphyxiation, her time was running out.

His body lurched from the impact at over ninety miles an hour, but he'd been ready, and although he was sore and probably had a few shattered ribs, he'd be fine. And the nose of the car was inside the warehouse. Right then, that was all that mattered.

He climbed out over the hood, then slid down to the ground, his eyes stinging as he searched for her.

He called her name, his throat and lungs burning, and heard nothing in reply.

Except...

He called again.

Yes.

He hurried across the warehouse, staying low, breathing shallow. The smoke was so thick he almost passed her, but he heard her soft, weak call. "Brax."

He spun left, then saw her. A wooden crate had fallen and her calf was trapped.

"I got loose," she said, her voice slow and tired. "Then something fell. Fucking Jorge."

Despite everything, he had to laugh at that.

He was already working on shifting the crate when Mason found them in the smoke. Between the two of them they managed to lift it, and they had to drag Sabrina—who'd fainted from either the pain or the smoke—out between them.

As they were exiting, four fire trucks pulled up, lights flashing. And in the moment that Brax looked back the way they came, the roof gave way, crushing everything below, including Old Blue.

Didn't matter. He had everything he needed in his arms, and he said a silent *thank you* to the car he'd loved.

"Hey," he said as her eyes fluttered open. He took a damp cloth one of the firefighters handed him and gently wiped her face. "You've had a pretty shitty day."

She laughed, then winced. "Don't. It hurts. My leg hurts, too."

"Yeah, it's seen better days. We'll get you fixed up."

"Okay." She smiled at him, as if certain he'd take care of everything.

He would.

"Baby? Can I ask you something?"

"Mm-hmm."

"Would you marry me?"

Her eyes fluttered open to meet his. "Yes," she said, her smile remaining as her eyes fluttered closed again.

He dipped his hand into his pocket and pulled out his mother's ring. Gently, he slipped it onto her finger. "We'll make it official later," he said as the arriving paramedics hurried over. "Right now, just know that you're mine."

We haven't even rung the doorbell when Ollie and Trevor open the door to their adorable house nestled in the canyons.

"You came," Ollie says, his smile wide. "I was afraid you weren't going to make it."

"Are you kidding? Miss your housewarming?" Brax shook his head. "Not in a million." He stepped inside and pulled Ollie into an awkward guy hug. "You ought to know better," he says. "Besides, Sabrina gets antsy when I don't take her out to enough social events."

"Jerk," I say, smacking him with my tiny purse.

"That's why I don't let her carry large purses," Brax says. I meet his eyes, and we both laugh.

"They're so freaking cute," Trevor says.

"I told you." Ollie says.

"Seriously," Trevor says, "you two look amazing."

"Well, it's been a crazy journey," Brax says. "But it was all worth it." He squeezes my hand, and we share a secret smile.

"And in another week, I won't need this," I say, tapping the cane. "Although I might pretend to. He's very skilled with the pampering," I say, tilting my head towards Brax. "I figure it might be fun to keep him on the hook."

"Very funny."

"I don't know," Trevor says. "Sounds like a good plan to me."

"You would say that," Ollie retorts. The four of us exchange glances, then laugh simultaneously.

We follow the guys further inside, and they show off the walls, the flooring, the work they did on the patio. All in all, the place is stunning. The view is absolutely spectacular, and nestled in the hills as it is, it feels like an extravagant tree house more than traditional construction. To be honest, I'm a little jealous. Brax and I have been talking about what kind of place we want, and I'm thinking that if we could get

Trevor and Ollie to give their place up, we'd be doing just fine.

Brax nudges me. "I know what you're thinking."

"If you think that I'm thinking that we need to send Ollie and Brax on a three-year-long tour of Europe so we can live in their house, then we definitely are on the same wavelength."

He laughs and squeezes my hand.

Ollie and Trevor drift off to get the door, and Brax points across the room to where Nikki and Damien Stark are standing. "We should go say hi," he says. I agree, and we start heading that direction. We get waylaid, though, when we see Cami standing to the side talking with Jamie Hunter. We detour that way, and she lights up when she sees us. Brax holds out his arms, then pulls her in for a hug.

She glances down at my cane, then back up to my face. "I'm so glad you weren't seriously hurt," she says.

"Me, too."

"And," I say, with a conspiratorial tone in my voice, "It's probably fair to say that the whole adventure that led to the mucking up of my leg also landed me Brax. So I really can't complain."

"No, I guess not," Cami says. "Did you hear that Ryan has an assignment for me? I guess that makes me official at Stark Security now."

I high-five her. "What's the assignment?" I ask.

"I don't know, but I hope it has something to do with tracking Lambert and the rest of the Group Ultra cells. He said he'd tell me at the office on Monday. Why do they do that? Now I'm going to be wondering all weekend."

"Well, I hope you're as lucky in your assignment as Brax was in his. After all, he got me back, didn't he?"

"That he did," Cami says, but without the teasing humor that I was expecting. "Although I don't know if that's really my kind of assignment."

"What do you mean?"

She doesn't answer, and I see Brax standing off to the side and giving me the evil eye. I squeeze Cami's hand, then make an excuse about searching for Trevor's famous chocolate chip cookies.

As I step away, Brax falls in beside me. "What was that about?" I ask.

"Cami doesn't do relationships," he says.

"Really? I thought you two slept together back in the day."

"Yeah, and that's all we did. No relationship. Friendship, yes. Relationship, no."

"Why?"

"I don't know," he says, his voice sounding a little bit far away and wistful. "To be honest, it's the one thing we've never talked about. I tried. I never succeeded."

I glance back at Cami and think about how lucky I am. I'm in a relationship with my best friend, who's also the man I love more than anything in the world. I can't imagine why she wouldn't want something like that, and I can only assume that someone hurt her so deeply in the past that she's gun-shy.

I hope that changes. That one day, she'll be lucky enough to fall in love with her best friend, too. I highly recommend it, after all.

A special note from JK:

I'm working on several projects now, both in and out of Stark World, and you can **read along as I write**!

How? By joining my **Patreon.**

For just $5/month you get to read the first draft of all the sexy, suspenseful, emotional goodness that comes off my keyboard and is on the path to being indie published! Plus even more perks, like exclusive stories for Patrons and a bonus "After the story" wrap up for *Entwined With You* coming next week!

(For a little bit more, you can even get digitally signed print editions of all the indie books I publish, ARCs, short stories, and more!)

Interested? Check out all the options and perks at JK's Patreon. Just visit Patreon.com/juliekenner

Want to be among the first to hear when Cami's story is available?

Visit www.juliekenner.com to sign up for her Elite Reader Group newsletter!

And keep reading for an excerpt from the *USA Today bestselling* WICKED GRIND!

WICKED GRIND

AN EXCERPT

A note from JK —

This erotic romance is one of my favorites! I
hope you enjoy this peek into a world where
passion, art, and pleasure mix in a way that is
decidedly, wonderfully steamy...

XXOO
Julie

PROLOGUE

I'd thought he was out of my life forever. That all that remained of him was a memory, sharp and forbidden. Terrifying, yet tempting.

The one man who changed everything.

The one night that destroyed my world.

I told myself I was past it. That I could see him again and not feel that tug. Not remember the hurt or the shame.

That's what I believed, anyway.

Honestly, I should have known better...

CHAPTER ONE

H*e was surrounded by naked women, and he was bored out of his mind.*

Wyatt Royce forced himself not to frown as he lowered his camera without taking a single shot. Thoughtfully, he took a step back, his critical eye raking over the four women who stood in front of him in absolutely nothing but their birthday suits.

Gorgeous women. Confident women. With luscious curves, smooth skin, bright eyes, and the kind of strong, supple muscles that left no doubt that each and every one of them could wrap their legs around a man and hold him tight.

In other words, each one had an erotic

allure. A glow. A certain *je ne sais quoi* that turned heads and left men hard.

None of them, however, had *it*.

"Wyatt? You ready, man?"

Jon Paul's voice pulled Wyatt from his frustrated thoughts, and he nodded at his lighting director. "Sorry. Just thinking."

JP turned his back to the girls before flashing a wolfish grin and lowering his voice. "I'll bet you were."

Wyatt chuckled. "Down, boy." Wyatt had hired the twenty-three year old UCLA photography grad student as a jack-of-all-trades six months ago. But when JP had proved himself to be not only an excellent photographer, but also a prodigy with lighting, the relationship had morphed from boss/assistant to mentor/protégé before finally holding steady at friend/colleague.

JP was damn good at his job, and Wyatt had come to rely on him. But JP's background was in architectural photography. And the fact that the female models he faced every day were not only gorgeous, but often flat-out, one hundred percent, provocatively nude, continued to be both a fascination to JP and, Wyatt suspected, the cause of a daily cold shower. Or three.

Not that Wyatt could criticize. After all, he was the one who'd manufactured the sensual, erotic world in which both he and JP spent their days. For months, he'd lost himself daily inside this studio, locked in with a series of stunning women, their skin warm beneath his fingers as he gently positioned them for the camera. Women eager to please. To move however he directed. To contort their bodies in enticing, tantalizing poses that were often unnatural and uncomfortable, and for no other reason than that he told them to.

As long as they were in front of his camera, Wyatt owned those women, fully and completely. And he'd be lying to himself if he didn't admit that in many ways the photo shoots were as erotically charged as the ultimate photographs.

So, yeah, he understood the allure, but he'd damn sure never succumbed to it. Not even when so many of his models had made it crystal clear that they were eager to move from his studio to his bedroom.

There was just too much riding on this project.

Too much? Hell, *everything* was riding on his upcoming show. His career. His life. His reputation. Not to mention his personal savings.

Eighteen months ago he'd set out to make a splash in the world of art and photography, and in just twenty-seven days, he'd find out if he'd succeeded.

What he hoped was that success would slam against him like a cannonball hitting water. So hard and fast that everybody in the vicinity ended up drenched, with him squarely at the center, the unabashed cause of all the commotion.

What he feared was that the show would be nothing more than a ripple, as if he'd done little more than stick his big toe into the deep end of the pool.

Behind him, JP coughed, the harsh sound pulling Wyatt from his thoughts. He glanced up, saw that each of the four women were staring at him with hope in their eyes, and felt like the ultimate heel.

"Sorry to keep you waiting, ladies. Just trying to decide how I want you." He spoke without any innuendo, but the petite brunette giggled anyway, then immediately pressed her lips together and dipped her gaze to the floor.

Wyatt pretended not to notice. "JP, go grab my Leica from my office. I'm thinking I want to shoot black and white."

He wasn't thinking that at all, not really. He was just buying time. Talking out of his ass while he decided what—if anything—to do with the girls.

As he spoke, he moved toward the women, trying to figure out why the hell he was so damned uninterested in all of them. Were they really that inadequate? So unsuited for the role he needed to fill?

Slowly, he walked around them, studying their curves, their angles, the soft glow of their skin under the muted lighting. This one had a haughty, aquiline nose. That one a wide, sensual mouth. Another had the kind of bedroom eyes that promised to fulfill any man's fantasies. The fourth, a kind of wide-eyed innocence that practically begged to be tarnished.

Each had submitted a portfolio through her agent, and he'd spent hours poring over every photograph. He had one slot left in the show. The centerpiece. The lynchpin. A single woman that would anchor all of his carefully staged and shot photos with a series of erotic images that he could already see clearly in his mind. A confluence of lighting and staging, of body and attitude. Sensuality coupled with innocence and underscored with daring.

He knew what he wanted. More than that, somewhere in the deep recesses of his mind, he even knew *who* he wanted.

So far, she hadn't wandered into his studio.

But she was out there, whoever she was; he was certain of it.

Too bad he only had twenty-seven days to find her.

Which was why he'd stooped to scouring modeling agencies, even though his vision for this show had always been to use amateur models. Women whose features or attitude caught his attention on the beach, in the grocery store, wherever he might be. Women from his past. Women from his work. But always women who didn't make a living with their bodies. That had been his promise to himself from the beginning.

And yet here he was, begging agents to send their most sensual girls to him. Breaking his own damn rule because he was desperate to find her. That elusive girl who was hiding in his mind, and who maybe—just maybe—had an agent and a modeling contract.

But he knew she wouldn't. Not that girl.

No, the girl he wanted would be a virgin with the camera, and he'd be the one who would first capture that innocence. That was his vision. The plan he'd stuck to for eighteen long months of squeezing in sessions between his regular commercial photography gigs. Almost two years of all-nighters in the dark room and surviving on coffee and protein bars because there wasn't time to order take-out, much less cook.

Months of planning and worrying and slaving toward a goal. And those sweet, precious moments when he knew—really knew—that he was on the verge of creating something truly spectacular.

He was exhausted, yes. But he was almost done.

So far, he had forty-one final images chosen for the show, each and every one perfect as far as he was concerned.

He just needed the final nine. That last set of photos of his one perfect woman. Photos that would finally seal his vision—both of the girl in his mind and of what he wanted to accomplish with this solo exhibition.

He'd sacrificed so much, and he was finally close. So damn close ... and yet here he was, spinning his wheels with models who weren't what he wanted or needed.

Fuck.

With a sigh of frustration, Wyatt dragged his fingers through his thick, short hair. "Actually, ladies, I think we're done here. I appreciate your time and your interest in the project, and I'll review your portfolios and be in touch with your agent if you're selected. You're free to get dressed and go."

The girls glanced at each other, bewildered. For that matter, JP looked equally puzzled as he returned to the studio with Wyatt's Leica slung over his shoulder and a tall, familiar redhead at his side.

"Siobhan," Wyatt said, ignoring the trepidation building in his gut. "I didn't realize we had a meeting scheduled."

"I thought you were going to shoot a roll of black and white," JP said at the same time, holding up the Leica in the manner of a third grader at Show-and-Tell.

In front of Wyatt, the girls paused in the act of pulling on their robes, obviously uncertain.

"We're done," Wyatt said to them before turning his attention to his assistant. "I have everything I need to make a decision."

"Right. Sure. You're the boss." But as JP spoke, he looked sideways at Siobhan, whose arms were now crossed over her chest, her brow furrowed with either confusion or annoyance. Quite probably both.

But Wyatt had to hand it to her; she held in her questions until the last model had entered the hallway that led to the dressing room, and the door had clicked shut behind her.

"You got what you needed?" she asked, cutting straight to the chase. "Does that mean one of those models is the girl you've been looking for?"

"Is that why you're here? Checking my progress?" *Shit.* He sounded like a guilty little boy standing in front of the principal.

Siobhan, thank God, just laughed. "One, I'm going to assume from the defensive tone that the answer is no. And two, I'm the director of your show first and foremost because we're friends. So take this in the spirit of friendship when I ask, what the hell are you doing? We have less than a month to pull all of this together. So if none of those girls is the one you need, then tell me what I can do to help. Because this is on me, too, remember? This show flops, and we both lose."

"Thanks," he said dryly. "I appreciate the uplifting and heartfelt speech."

"Screw uplifting. I want you on the cover of every art and photography magazine in the country, with your show booked out on loan to at least a dozen museums and galleries for the next five years. I couldn't care less if you're uplifted. I just want you to pull this off."

"Is that all?" he asked, fighting a smile.

"Hell no. I also want a promotion. My boss is considering moving to Manhattan. I covet her office."

"Good to have a goal," JP said, tilting his head toward Wyatt. "I covet his."

"Go," Wyatt said, waving his thumb toward the dressing room. "Escort the girls out through the gallery," he ordered. The space was divided into his two-story studio that boasted a discreet entrance off the service alley, and a newly remodeled gallery and storefront that opened onto one of Santa Monica's well-trafficked retail areas.

"So you're really done?" JP pressed. "That's it? Not even a single shot?"

"I don't need to see anything else," Wyatt said. "Go. Chat them up so they don't feel like they wasted their time. And then I'll see you tomorrow."

"That's your subtle way of getting rid of me, isn't it?"

"Don't be ridiculous," Wyatt retorted. "I wasn't being subtle at all."

JP smirked, but didn't argue. And with a wave to Siobhan, he disappeared into the back hallway.

"So how can I help?" Siobhan asked once he was gone. "Should I arrange a round of auditions? After all, I know a lot of really hot women."

That was true enough. In fact, Siobhan's girlfriend, Cassidy, featured prominently in the show. And it had been through Cass that Wyatt had originally met Siobhan, who had both a background in art and a shiny new job as the assistant director of the Stark Center for the Visual Arts in downtown Los Angeles.

Originally, Wyatt had envisioned a significantly smaller show staged in his studio. The location was good, after all, and he anticipated a lot of foot traffic since folks could walk from the Third Street Promenade. He'd asked Cass to model about eight months ago, not only because she was stunning, but because he knew the flamboyant tattoo artist well enough to know that she wouldn't balk at any pose he came up with, no matter how provocative. Cass didn't have a shy bone in her body, and she was more than happy to shock—so long as the shock was delivered on her terms.

Siobhan had come with her, and before the shoot, Wyatt had shown both of them three of the pieces he'd already finished so that Cass would have a sense of his vision. It was the first time he'd laid it out in detail, and it had been cathartic talking to Siobhan, who spoke the language, and Cass, who was an artist herself, albeit one whose canvas was skin and whose tools were ink and needles.

He'd explained how he'd originally just wanted a break from the portraits and other commercial photography jobs that paid the bills. And, yes, he was beginning to make a name for himself artistically with his landscapes and city scenes. That success was gratifying, but ultimately unsatisfying because those subjects weren't his passion. There was beauty in nature, sure, but Wyatt wanted to capture physical, feminine eroticism on film.

More than that, he wanted to make a statement, to tell a story. Beauty. Innocence. Longing. Ecstasy. He wanted to look at the world through the eyes of these women, and the women through the eyes of the world.

Ultimately, he wanted to elevate erotic art. To use it to reveal more about the models than even they were aware. Strength and sensuality. Innocence and power. Passion and gentleness. He envisioned using a series of provocative, stunning images to manipulate the audience through the story of the show, sending them on a journey from innocence to debauchery and back again, and then leaving them breathless with desire and wonder.

That afternoon, Wyatt spoke with Cass and Siobhan for over an hour. Showing them examples. Describing the emotions he wanted to evoke. Listening to their suggestions, and taking satisfaction from the fact that they obviously loved the concept. They'd ended the conversation with Cass posing for another hour as he burned through three rolls of film, certain he was capturing some of his best work yet.

Then they'd walked to Q, a Santa Monica

restaurant and bar known for its martini flights. They'd toasted his project, Cass's pictures, and Siobhan's career, and by the time they ended the evening, he was feeling pretty damn good about his little pet project.

The next morning, he'd felt even better. That's when Siobhan had come to him with a formal offer from the Stark Center. He'd said yes on the spot, never once thinking that by doing so he was tying another person to his success—or, more to the point, his potential failure.

"I'm serious," she pressed now, as his silence continued to linger. "Whatever you need."

"I'll find her," Wyatt said. "I have time."

"Not much," she countered. "I need the prints ahead of time for the catalog, not to mention installation. Keisha's already getting twitchy," she added, referring to her boss. "We don't usually cut it this close."

"I know. It's going to be—"

"Twenty-seven days to the show, Wyatt." He could hear the tension in her voice, and hated himself for being the cause of it. "But about half that before you need to deliver the prints. We're running out of time. If you can't find the girl, then you need to just find *a* girl. I'm sorry, but—"

"I said I'll find her. You have to trust me on this."

Right then, she didn't look like she'd trust him to take care of her goldfish, but to her credit, she nodded. "Fine. In that case, all I need today is to see the latest print so I can think about the promotional image. And you'll email me a file for the catalog?"

"Sure. This is it," he added, walking to a covered canvas centered on the nearest wall. He pulled down the white drape, revealing a life-size black and white photograph of a woman getting dressed. At first glance, it wasn't the most titillating of his images, but that was because it was such a tease. The woman stood in a dressing room, and hidden among the dresses and coats were at least a dozen men, peering out to watch her.

The woman, however, was oblivious. She was bending over, one foot on a stool, as she fastened a garter. The view was at an angle, so at first glance the audience saw only her skirt, a hint of garter, and the woman's silk-sheathed leg.

Then they noticed the mirror behind her. A

mirror that revealed that she wasn't wearing panties under the garter belt. And even though absolutely nothing was left to the imagination, it still wasn't a particularly racy or erotic photograph. But then you noticed the reflection in the mirror of another mirror. And another. And another. Each with an image of that same woman, and each slightly more risqué, until finally, as the mirror approached infinity, the woman was nude, her head thrown back, one hand between her legs, the other at her throat. And all those men from the closet were out in the open now, their hands stroking and teasing her.

Most important, the mirror was so deep in the image that you had to stand practically nose-to-print to see it.

Wyatt couldn't wait to see how many people did exactly that at the showing.

"This is fabulous," Siobhan said with genuine awe in her voice.

"It was a hell of a photograph to set up and then develop. Lots of work on the set and in the darkroom."

"You could have set it up digitally."

He scoffed. "No. Some of the images, sure. But not this one." He turned his head, regarding it critically. "This one had to be hands-on. It's as much about the process as the product."

"Yeah. I get that." She met his eyes, and the respect in hers reminded him of why he didn't just take photos for himself. "I want to take it back with me right now and show Keisha," she added.

"Soon." Although Siobhan and Keisha had wanted him to deliver each print upon completion, Wyatt had balked, explaining that he needed the art surrounding him in order to ensure the continuity of story in the overall exhibit. And the size of the canvas and the particulars of the way he handled the image in the darkroom were such that duplicates weren't adequate.

That meant that when Siobhan needed to see a piece, she came to him. And now that she was not only putting together the official catalog, but also doing promotional pieces from the images, she was coming a lot.

Wyatt was adamant that the images not be revealed prior to the show, but Siobhan's team had promised him the rapidly expanding catalog mockup would be kept under lock and key. More important, the pre-show promotion wouldn't reveal any of the artwork—while at the same time, teasing the art's sensual and daring nature.

So far, they'd not only managed to do just that, but the campaign was already a success. The gallery had been releasing one image a month— one of his photographs, yes, but only a sexy snippet shown through a virtual barrier laid over the image. Once, it was yellow *caution* tape. Another time, it was a keyhole in a hotel room door. Clever, yes, but also effective. Wyatt had already been interviewed and the exhibit pimped out in no less than five local papers and magazines. And he was booked on two morning shows the day the exhibit opened.

Not bad, all things considered, and he told Siobhan as much.

"If you really want to see a bump in our publicity," she replied, "we should get your grandmother on board."

"No." The word came swift and firm.

"Wyatt..."

"I said no. This exhibit is on my shoulders. I can't hide who I am, but I don't have to advertise it. If we trot my grandmother out, book her on morning shows, make her sing little Wyatt's praises, then everyone is going to come. You know that."

"Um, yeah. That's the point. To get people to your show."

"I want them to come for the show. Not because they're hoping to get Anika Segel's autograph."

"But they'll see your art. They'll fall in love then. Who cares what brings them through the door?"

"I do," he said and was relieved to see that she didn't seem to have an argument against that.

She stood still for a moment, possibly trying to come up with something, but soon enough she shook her head and sighed. "You're the artist." She made a face. "And you have the temperament to go with it."

"See, that's how you wooed me into doing the show with you. That embarrassingly senti-mental flattery."

"You're a laugh a minute, Wyatt." She hitched her purse further onto her shoulder, then pointed a finger at him. "Don't fuck this up."

"Cross my heart."

"All right then." She leaned in for an air kiss, but caught him in a hug. "It's going to be great," she whispered, and he was surprised by how much he appreciated those simple words.

"It will," he agreed. "All I have to do is find the girl." He glanced at his watch. "An agency's sending someone over in about half an hour. Nia. Mia. Something like that. Who knows? Maybe she'll be the one."

"Fingers crossed." Her grin turned wicked. "But if she's not, just say the word and Cass and I will dive into the search."

"A few more days like today, and I'll take you up on that."

"A few days is all you have," she retorted, then tossed up her hands, self-defense style. "I know, I know. I'm leaving."

She headed for the front door, and he turned back to the print, studying it critically. A moment later he reached for the drapes that covered the prints on either side of the first image, then tugged them off, revealing the full-color photos beneath.

He took a step back as he continued his inspection, ensuring himself that there were no more refinements to be made. Slowly, he moved farther back, wanting all three in his field of vision, just like a visitor to the exhibition would see. One step, then another and another.

He stopped when he heard the door open behind him, cursing himself for not locking up as Siobhan was leaving. "Did you forget something?" he asked as he turned.

But it wasn't Siobhan.

It was *her*.

The girl who'd filled his mind. The girl who'd haunted his nights.

The woman he needed if he was going to pull this exhibit off the way he wanted to.

A woman with the kind of wide sensual mouth that could make a man crazy, and a strong, lithe body, with curves in all the right places. Eyes that could see all the way into a man's soul—and an innocent air that suggested she wouldn't approve of what she saw there.

All of that, topped off with a wicked little tease of a smile and a sexy swing to her hips.

She was a walking contradiction. Sensual yet demure. Sexy yet sweet.

A woman who one minute could look like a cover model, and the next like she'd never done anything more glamorous than walk the dog.

She was hotter than sin, and at the same time she was as cold as ice.

She was Kelsey Draper, and he hadn't spoken to her since the summer before his senior year, and as far as he was concerned, that was a damn good thing.

Her eyes widened as she looked at him, and her lips twitched in a tremulous smile. "Oh," was all she said.

And in that moment, Wyatt knew that he was well and truly screwed.

CHAPTER TWO

O*h.*
        The word seems to hang above us inside a cartoon bubble, and I mentally cringe. Ten years at an exclusive girls' school, an under-graduate degree in early education, minors in both dance and English, and the best I can come up with is *Oh?*

And, yes, I know I should cut myself a little slack. After all, I was caught off guard. Not by the stunning and sensual art displayed in front of me, but by the man who created it. A man who's the reason my palms are sweaty, my nipples tight, and my pulse beating a staccato rhythm in my neck.

A man I once knew as Wyatt Segel.

A man I was completely unprepared to see.

Which means that Nia has some serious explaining to do. *"Just some photographer looking for models. My agent says the pay is awesome, and considering how much cash you need by the end of the month, it's worth a shot. He goes by W. Royce, but I've never heard of the guy. Then again, who cares so long as he pays?"*

Never heard of the guy? Oh, please. Nia's a model; Wyatt's a photographer. She must have known he'd taken a stage name. And then she went and set me up.

Honestly, I just might have to kill her.

First, though, I have to get this job. My brother Griffin's a fourth degree burn survivor, and I have less than a month to come up with fifteen thousand dollars in order to enroll him in trials for an innovative new clinical protocol. Not an easy task on my kindergarten teacher salary, and even the additional dance classes I've added to my summer teaching schedule don't come close to taking up the monetary slack.

Which is why when my best friend Nia told me about the audition, it seemed worth the shot. Granted, I took some convincing. And I wasn't entirely comfortable with the idea of putting myself on display. But I psyched myself up. Desperate times, and all that.

"My agent booked me for a lingerie shoot," she'd told me over drinks on the balcony of her beachfront condo yesterday. "A last minute gig. I guess the photographer's pushing up against his deadline. Anyway, I think you should go in my place. His name's W. Royce, and I can text you the address and time."

My stomach lurched at the thought. "Are you crazy? I can't do that!"

Nia sighed dramatically. "Why? Because it would be *wrong*?" She put finger quotes around the last word.

"Actually, yes," I said adamantly. Nia constantly teases me about what she calls my elevated sense of scruples. She's convinced that I'm too staid and regimented. That I need to deviate from my safe little routine and cut loose sometimes. But she's one hundred percent wrong about that.

I know better than anyone the price you pay when you break the rules.

"He'll be expecting a drop-dead gorgeous woman who oozes sensuality," I said pragmatically. "And that's really not me."

"Oh, honey, please. We both know you're gorgeous. And where else are you going to get that kind of money so quickly? Especially since you're too stubborn to borrow from me."

"You're assuming I'll get the job." Unlike Nia, who's been modeling since she was seven, I have absolutely zero experience.

"Did I mention you're gorgeous? Just because you never flaunt it, doesn't mean it's not true."

I crossed my arms to hide an involuntary shudder. She's wrong, of course. Not about me being pretty—I am. And that's a cross I've had to bear my entire life.

No, she was wrong about the rest of it. Because I did flaunt it. Maybe not much—and only once—but that was enough, and I opened a Pandora's Box of badness that I'm still trying to close.

I licked my lips, my thoughts turning to my brother. That photographer might be pushing a deadline, but so was I. And if there was even the tiniest chance that this job could get me the cash I needed, then didn't I at least owe it to Griffin to try? Maybe under normal circumstances, lingerie modeling would be too racy for my sensibilities. But these weren't ordinary circumstances.

"I can't do sexy photos. I wouldn't have a

clue how to pose," I said, but my protest lacked oomph, and I saw from the way Nia's eyes lit up that she knew I'd taken the bait, and all she had to do was reel me in.

"It's just commercial lingerie photos," she shrugged as if to say that was no big deal. "Just pretend you're at the beach in a bikini."

I considered that, then nodded. It's not like I've never displayed a little skin. And I do own a bikini. I even wear it on the beach. In public. Sometimes.

And after everything that happened back then, wasn't there some sort of karmic justice in me stripping down to my underwear for a good cause? I didn't know, but it sounded like a solid justification to me.

"Besides," Nia continued, "a professional photographer's going to have an excellent bedside manner."

"Nia!"

"Oh, for fuck's sake, Kels. It's a figure of speech."

"Language."

"Fuckety, fuck, fuck, fuck," she retorted. And I couldn't help myself—I burst out laughing. "Love me, love my potty mouth," she said.

"I do love you," I admitted. "*Despite* the potty mouth."

"That's because I'm so damn, fucking lovable." She flashed a wicked grin before taking another sip of wine while I tried hard not to laugh again. Best not to egg her on.

"Seriously, Kels, it'll be easy. It's a lot like dancing. Form and position and movement. In a lot of ways modeling is like choreography. And I've seen the outfits you rehearse in. Not a lot left to the imagination, right?"

"That's different." When I dance, I dress for comfort and ease of movement. More to the point, I let myself become someone else, someone in tune with the euphoria of the music. Someone willing to let go of control, because the thread of the music is always there to pull me back and keep me safe.

"Quit arguing and just go for it. Trust me, this job will be good for you. You can get your naughty on in a baby step kind of way, and all the while you can tell yourself you're only doing it because of Griffin. It's perfect."

"First of all, I *am* only doing it for Griffin. I'm not looking for excuses to wear a tiny bikini or flash my breasts. I like me. I like my life. I'm happy. I'm comfortable with who I am."

"Methinks the lady doth protest too much."

"Oh, give me a break," I snapped, feeling unreasonably defensive. "I don't need to hop in bed with a guy on the first date or—"

"First date? Try fifth. Or never. And for that matter, when was the last time you even went on a date?"

"That's not the point," I said, because it really wasn't. "There just aren't many guys out there that interest me. And why should I go to dinner or drinks with a total dud, much less sleep with him? And you're getting off the subject," I added.

She held up her hands. "You're the one who started talking about dating. My point was only that you should take the job because you need the money—but that you should try to have a good time, too."

I took a long swallow and finished off my wine. "All I care about is getting enough money to enroll Griffin in the protocol."

"Sure. Right. You justify it however you want. The point is, this is a rock solid deal. At the very least, you owe it to yourself—and Griffin—to go to the audition."

I think about that conversation now, as I stand in Wyatt's studio in the shadow of these sensual, shocking photos. Photos that terrify me, taken by a man who excites me.

I think about it, and I want to run.

But I can't. Because Nia was right. I have to do this. I have to land this job.

All of which means that I have to ace this audition, Wyatt or no Wyatt. And that will probably go a lot better if I can actually conjure words. Which, considering how many times I've imagined bumping into him, is turning out to be surprisingly difficult.

In my head, I'm always clever and amusing during our imaginary encounters in bookstores and restaurants. And when we're assigned as seatmates on the long journey from Los Angeles to Australia, I'm not the least bit tongue-tied.

Not that I've ever actually flown to Australia, but I've spent the better part of my life playing out a variety of fantasies in my head. And what's the point of fantasy if you can't fix past mistakes? If you can't be someone a little different than who you are? Especially if there's no way in hell you'd take the leap in real life?

Over the last twelve years, I've spun infinite variations on my Wyatt fantasy. Sometimes we barely speak two words. Sometimes, I'll let him buy me a drink. Once or twice, I let it go a little bit further. But even in my fantasies, I can't bring myself to give us a happily ever after.

Because between Wyatt and me, the story is a tragedy, not a romance. Considering everything that happened, how could it be anything else?

Now, Wyatt is nothing more than a pushpin in the map of my life. A reminder of how horrible things can get, and why bad choices are, as advertised, *bad*.

He's not a man, he's a concept. A talisman. Fantasy mixed with memory and topped with a sprinkle of loss.

Unfortunate, maybe, but at least *that's* a Wyatt I can handle.

But this Wyatt? The one standing in front of me with golden-brown hair and whiskey-colored eyes that can see all the way into our past. The one whose lean body I can still imagine pressed against me, and whose strong arms once made me feel safe. The one with the impudent grin that used to make my heart flutter, but who now isn't smiling at all.

The boy who once made my breath catch in my throat whenever I caught a glimpse of him. Who's now a man who walks with confidence and grace and commands a room simply by standing in it.

The boy who made me break all the rules. Who made me lose control.

The man who nearly destroyed me.

That man isn't manageable at all. On the contrary, that man terrifies me. And right now, I can't help but think that coming on this audition was a mistake of monumental proportions.

Yup. Definitely going to have to kill Nia. A pity, really. Because when am I going to find the time to go shopping for a new best friend?

More important, how else am I going to earn fifteen grand by the end of the month?

As I stand there like a dolt, he crosses his arms over his chest and tilts his head just slightly. That's when I realize that he's been watching me all this time. Not saying a word. Just waiting. As if this is all on me.

I guess maybe it is.

I swallow, forcing myself not to dry my sweaty palms on my gray pencil skirt as I smile tentatively. I watch his face, hoping for an answering grin. For some hint that he's thought of me over the last twelve years. A sign that he remembers the things we said, the way we laughed. The way we touched.

I wait for even the tiniest inkling that I have lingered in his mind the way that he's lingered in mine. Because he has. Even when everything was screwed up and horrible. Even after I ruined everything. Even when I knew I shouldn't, I still thought of him.

And now, like a damn beggar, I'm searching his face for some sign that he's thought of me, too.

But there's nothing to see.

Right. Fine. Okay.

I let my gaze shift to the walls, but that's a mistake because I'm immediately drawn to the three uncovered photographs hanging behind him. They're raw and titillating, disturbing and honest. I can feel them resonate inside me, firing my blood and causing a flurry of pleasant-yet-terrifying sparks to zing around inside me.

I quickly turn my attention back to Wyatt and clear my throat. "So," I say, trying to speak normally. "Usually I'm auditioning to dance, not model. What do you want me to do?"

A heat so quick it could be my imagination flashes as his eyes narrow more, and I see a subtle tightening in his jaw. "Kelsey," he finally says, and the sound of my name on his lips sends a wave of relief coursing through me. At the very least, I know he remembers me.

"Yeah." I smile brightly, then remember that this is supposed to be an audition. I've been clutching a headshot with my email address and cell number on it, and I scurry forward and thrust it at him. "It's me."

He doesn't even look at it.

"It's been a long time." His voice is flat. Even.

"It has," I agree, my voice so sing-song I feel like an idiot. But he doesn't seem to hear me. Instead, he's looking me up and down, the slow inspection as sensual as a hand moving leisurely up my body. I draw in a breath and feel it flutter in my throat. My skin tingles with awareness, and I can feel small beads of sweat rise at the base of my neck, thankfully hidden under my shoulder-length chestnut waves.

I force myself not to shift my weight from foot to foot. It's hard, because right now I feel as exposed as the models in the photographs gracing the walls behind him. And when Wyatt's eyes finally meet mine, and his inspection ceases, I'm positive that my cheeks have bloomed a bright, revealing red.

I draw another breath in anticipation of his

words. I expect him to say something about our past. At the very least, to say that it's good to see me after so much time.

I couldn't be more wrong.

"What the hell are you doing here?" he demands, and it's as if he's tossed a bucket of cold water all over me.

I sputter. I actually sputter as a chill runs through me, and I struggle to recover my thoughts, my power of speech, my pride. "I—I just ... well, the job."

I stand straighter, fighting a fresh wave of vulnerability. Because Wyatt is dangerous to me, and I really need to keep that little fact at the forefront of my mind. "I'm here about the job," I repeat, and this time my voice is crisp and clear.

He pulls out his phone, taps the screen, then looks back at me with a frown. "Nia Hancock. Twenty-seven. Mixed race female. Her agent called yesterday and said he was sending her over."

I lick my lips. "She, um, couldn't come. And since I could use the job, I came in her place."

"You came?" he repeats, and I watch as a series of expressions crosses his face, starting with surprise, then moving into confusion, and settling on something that looks remarkably like anger. "You?" His voice takes on a bland tone that is more than a little disconcerting.

I open my mouth to answer, but he continues before I can get a word in edgewise.

"You expect me to believe that Kelsey Draper wants to be a model. One of these models?" he adds, waving a hand behind him to indicate the three uncovered paintings, larger than life in so many ways.

I lick my lips, then immediately regret the unconscious action. Because I'm not sure. I'm really not sure at all.

Then I remember Griffin. And the money. And the fact that I'm desperate.

And, yes, I think about those scary-but-tantalizing sparks that are zinging around in my bloodstream. I shouldn't want it. In fact, I should hightail it right out that door before everything crashes down on me again.

But I don't. Instead, I glance down at the floor and murmur, "Yes. That's exactly what I want."

He's silent, so I lift my chin, hoping he can see my resolve, but there's nothing warm or welcoming in his expression. On the contrary, what I see on his face is anger. And when he scoffs and says, "What the hell kind of game are you playing this time?" I know that I've made a terrible, horrible, awful mistake.

"I'm not playing a game," I protest, but my voice comes out shaky instead of strong. "It's just that I need—"

"What?" he demands. "What could you possibly need from me?"

The harshness in his voice slices through me, and I cringe. I want to explain myself, but when I feel the tears well in my eyes, I know that there's no way I can hold myself together. "I'm sorry," I whisper as I turn to flee. "I should never have come here at all."

ABOUT THE AUTHOR

J. Kenner (aka Julie Kenner) is the *New York Times, USA Today, Publishers Weekly, Wall Street Journal* and #1 International bestselling author of over one hundred novels, novellas and short stories in a variety of genres.

JK has been praised by *Publishers Weekly* as an author with a "flair for dialogue and eccentric characterizations" and by *RT Bookclub* for having "cornered the market on sinfully attractive, dominant antiheroes and the women who swoon for them." A six-time finalist for Romance Writers of America's prestigious RITA award, JK took home the first RITA trophy awarded in the category of erotic romance in 2014 for her novel, *Claim Me* (book 2 of her Stark Saga) and another RITA trophy for *Wicked Dirty* in the same category in 2017.

In her previous career as an attorney, JK worked as a lawyer in Southern California and Texas. She currently lives in Central Texas, with her husband, two daughters, and two rather spastic cats.

Stay in touch! Text JKenner to 21000 to subscribe to JK's text alerts and visit www.jkenner.com to connect through social media!

Printed in the USA
CPSIA information can be obtained
at www.ICGtesting.com
LVHW011754221023
761812LV00003B/90

9 781958 379141